Good Knights

Other titles from St. Augustine's Press & Dumb Ox Books

Written by Ralph McInerny

Some Catholic Writers
The Defamation of Pius XII
Shakespearean Variations
The Soul of Wit
Let's Read Latin

Translation by Ralph McInerny

John of St. Thomas, *Introduction to the Summa Theologiae of Thomas Aquinas*

Thomas Aquinas, *Disputed Questions on Virtue*

Florent Gaboriau, *The Conversion of Edith Stein*

Introduction or Preface by Ralph McInerny

Thomas Aquinas, *Commentary on Aristotle's De Anima*

Thomas Aquinas, *Commentary on Aristotle's Metaphysics*

Thomas Aquinas, *Commentary on Aristotle's Nicomachean Ethics*

Thomas Aquinas, *Commentary on Aristotle's Physics*

Thomas Aquinas, *Commentary on Aristotle's Posterior Analytics*

Josef Pieper, *The Silence of Goethe*

Fulvio di Blasi, *God and the Natural Law*

Other Titles of Interest

James V. Schall, *The Regensburg Lecture*

Josef Pieper, *Happiness and Contemplation*

Josef Pieper, *The Silence of St. Thomas*

Josef Pieper, *What Catholics Believe*

C.S. Lewis, *The Latin Letters of C.S. Lewis*

Rémi Brague, *Eccentric Culture: A Theory of Western Civilization*

Peter Kreeft, *The Philosophy of Jesus*

Jacques Maritain, *Natural Law: Reflections on Theory and Practice*

GOOD KNIGHTS

Eight Stories

Ralph McInerny

St. Augustine's Press

South Bend, Indiana

2010

Manufactured in the United States of America.

1 2 3 4 5 6   16 15 14 13 12 11 10

Library of Congress Cataloging in Publication Data
McInerny, Ralph M.
Good Knights: eight stories / Ralph McInerny.
p. cm.
ISBN-13: 978-1-58731-335-6 (hardbound: alk. paper)
ISBN-10: 1-58731-335-9 (hardbound: alk. paper)
1. Brothers – Fiction. 2. Private investigators – Fiction.
3. College teachers – Fiction. 4. South Bend (Ind.) – Fiction.
5. Notre Dame (Ind.) – Fiction. 6. Detective and mystery
stories, American. I. Title.
PS3563.A31166G66 2009
813'.54 – dc22   2009024039

∞ *The paper used in this publication meets the minimum
requirements of the American National Standard for
Information Sciences – Permanence of Paper for Printed
Materials, ANSI Z39.48-1984.*

St. Augustine's Press
www.staugustine.net

For Jonathan Michiels

CONTENTS

PREFACE

Roger Knight and his brother Phil put in cameo appearances in *The Noonday Devil* and some readers were kind enough to tell me how much they enjoyed them, particularly Roger. So I put them into *Easeful Death* as well. There are characters about whom it is easy to write, sometimes fatally so, and Roger Knight is one of them for me. That is why I needed an exterior response to assure myself that I wasn't simply engaged in self-indulgence in writing about him. Perhaps Roger would have intruded into other later novels. But that was not to be.

After I brought Father Dowling to Notre Dame in one of the novels of the series that features him, sales soared. My publisher decided that the inclusion of Notre Dame was the explanation and I was urged to move Father Dowling permanently to the campus. Well, I couldn't do that. The trip to Notre Dame was a rare excursion for Father Dowling. His permanent place is St. Hilary's parish in Fox River, Illinois, and there is sufficient mischief there to keep him occupied. To move him elsewhere, save temporarily, would have been a violation of his character. So I made a counter proposal. I would begin another series, set on the campus of Notre Dame.

A series needs a sleuth, of course, a recurrent character who is sufficiently interesting to bring the reader and the author, back to him again and again. So I began to imagine characters for a Notre Dame series. Every time I came up with a halfway interesting possibility I had an uneasy sense of *déjà vu*. I realized I was imagining variations on Roger Knight. There was only one solution. Bring Roger Knight and his brother to Notre Dame.

At the time, I was still editing *Crisis*, the magazine Michael Novak and I had founded, and I decided to do a series of short stories for that magazine, finger exercises, so to speak, getting more familiar with Roger and his brother. The result was the eight stories gathered here. They are what they are and not another thing, as Bishop Butler said. The response to them was kind, but for me they were just the warm-up I needed before starting the new series. In them, Roger and his brother are living in Rye, New York, whither they have repaired from Manhattan and from which Philip operates as a private detective with Roger's assistance. From there I took them to Notre Dame.

The new series began with *On This Rockne* in 1996 and there has been another entry every year since. Most of them have atrocious puns for titles – *Lack of the Irish, Emerald Aisle, Irish Tenure, The Book of Kills* – you get the idea. You can get them all in almost any library and, as for the current one, in better bookstores everywhere, or on Amazon.com. While Roger is the same age in the thirteenth novel as he was in the first, the campus on which the action takes place has changed almost beyond recognition. I sometimes think that these stories will have some historical value because of this.

Devoted readers – both of them – will notice Roger develop through these stories, not yet the character in the later series, but with, shall I say, a family resemblance. His earlier selves in the novels mentioned above are reasonably identical with the one who now moves about the Notre Dame campus in his golf cart, wonderfully obese, and wiser than his creator. I mean of course his author. May they afford some hours of pleasure to you.

1

Fall of Man[1]

Given his enormous size, Roger Knight was capable of discomfort in any season, with the result that he had come to appreciate them all, but the winter scene at their window suggested to his brother Philip the ultimate level of hell.

"I'll show you the Doré illustrations of Dante to prove it."

Roger ignored him. He had been seated on a couch facing the expanse of the front lawn as it went out to their fence along the road and now he sat forward.

"When did it stop snowing, Phil?"

"Who said it stopped?" But Roger had heaved himself to his feet and now stood at the window, blotting out the light.

"We had a visitor during the night." The trail led up along the road and then detoured across the lawn in the direction of the barn. Philip, standing next to

1 A Roger Knight Mystery, by Ralph McInerny, *Crisis* Magazine, February 1997

him now, observed that the footprints were all but covered over.

"The wind makes it hard to know how fresh they are.

"We better check, Phil."

"The tracks could go right on into the woods."

But they did not. The door of the shed beside the barn had been opened and shut during the night, leaving a fanlike tracing on the snow. From the back porch, Roger watched his brother, booted now, the hood of his coat pulled over his head, move cautiously toward the barn. The shed did not open easily. Phil peered in, after having first thrust his flashlight into the unlit interior. With a cry, he disappeared inside.

Roger had let himself gingerly down the steps toward the snowy walk when Philip emerged from the shed, carrying someone in his arms. He shouted to Roger to go back inside, but his attention was to his footing and to the burden he bore with the gentleness of St. Christopher himself. It was a boy, perhaps eight years old, half-frozen and more than half-asleep. He groaned slightly when Phil lay him on the couch. Roger was busy at the fireplace, trying to get it started.

"Better let me, Roger. You'll blow us all up. Is there any oatmeal left?"

"Good idea."

The oatmeal was a concoction of Roger's, loaded with raisins and maple sugar and covered with cream. He carried it with devotion into the living room, where the boy had stirred awake. He looked warily from Philip to Roger.

"What's your name?" Philip asked, but his tone was that of a truant officer. Roger elbowed him aside and pulled up a hassock and perched upon it. Roger aimed a spoonful of oatmeal at the boy's mouth, who opened it in self-defense. In minutes, the bowl was empty.

"More?"

The boy nodded and got into a seated position. "I don't want to go back."

Roger ignored him. "How about some cinnamon toast with your next bowl? Tell you what, come out to the kitchen so I don't have to carry things."

The boy slid off the coach and followed Roger into the kitchen, where he was installed at the table and fed until he could eat no more. A single slice of bacon remained on the platter and Roger, convinced that the boy was full, picked it up and ate it.

"Waste not, want not. Where is it you don't want to go back to?"

"They say it's home but it isn't. And he isn't my father either. I hate him."

By seeming to give the boy only half his attention, Roger elicited the story. He had run away from a house a mile to the north that his mother and "new father" had recently bought. He had been taken there from his real father. Roger shook his head sadly. Half the marriages in the country were said to end in divorce and this youngster was one of the casualties of the cavalier attitude toward the marriage bond.

"What's your new father's name?" Philip asked, his tone softer this time.

A long pause.

"Henry."

"What's yours?"

"Chris."

Roger smiled, remembering how he had thought of St. Christopher when Phil came carrying the boy from the barn.

His name was Chris Dolan, and Dolan was his real father's name as well. He had trouble remembering the name of the man his mother had now married, but finally it came out. Carter. While Roger put Chris to work, helping with the breakfast dishes, Phil put on a coat and went off to locate Henry Carter.

Roger and Chris were sitting at the computer, surfing the web, when the phone rang. It was Phil.

"Any luck?" Roger asked in neutral tones.

"He's dead, Roger. Henry Carter is dead."

As a private detective, Philip Knight was used to dismissive treatment from the police, but Timmy Polk, the town constable, had been relieved when Phil arrived at the Carter house. Polk told him what he knew, which wasn't much. Mrs. Carter had called 911, crying that her husband had been murdered. The body lay in an unheated porch on the north side of the house, face down, the thick hair matted with blood from a wound in the head. Mortimer, the coroner, was examining the body, his breathing visible in the frigid air, his nose twitching like a rabbit's, his expression impassive. Some bodies are alive, others are dead. This was one of the dead ones.

After calling Roger, Phil looked over the scene more carefully. The body was stiff as a board and the wound seemed cauterized by the cold. He closed his eyes in order to retain the scene so he could describe it to Roger. Marie Carter's hysterical grief turned to hysterical joy when Phil told her that her son was safe. She hadn't realized he was missing until she found her husband's body and immediately went to check on Chris. Of course she thought whoever had murdered her husband had kidnapped her son. Polk had one of his deputies drive her off to the Knights.

"She was married to a man named Dolan," Polk said. "He's the kid's father."

"I'll check him out if you like."

"I thought the kid was with your brother?"

Phil said, "I was thinking of the body."

Polk got the point. The former husband did not have to be a kidnapper in order to be a murderer. "You're deputized, Knight. I mean that."

Phil laughed if off. Working hand in glove with the constable was one thing, but he did not want to relinquish his freelance status. He left his car at the Carter house and went slowly down the drive and then along the road. He was following tracks like the ones Roger had noticed across their lawn. About fifty yards from the Carter house, Phil stopped, knelt and brushed away the snow. A hammer came into view. There was hair mingled with the blood that had congealed on it.

Home again, Phil took Roger aside and told him about the hammer.

"And you were following Chris's tracks?"

"Yes."

"Where is the hammer?"

"I left it there." From the other room came the sound of Chris chattering to his mother. The significance of the hammer thrown aside along the route that the boy had taken to their house seemed inescapable, and Phil was plunged into sadness. His promise to go see Chris's father seemed a kind of escape.

"I'll check out the hammer," Roger whispered.

Jeffrey Dolan, M.D., reacted to the news of Carter's murder by just widening his eyes, but then he sat forward, his stethoscope banging against the desk. "How is Chris?"

Philip assured him that his son was safe. "He and his mother are at our place, just up the road. My brother Roger will look after them."

"Did you say you're a detective?"

"Yes."

"In the constable's office?"

"I'm a private detective."

Dolan lay his manicured hands flat on the desk. His shirt was immaculate and stiffly starched; as for his tie, Roger would have called it piebald. The physician's eyes held Philip's.

"I want to hire you. I want you to find the man who killed Carter."

Philip had not come seeking employment and he doubted that Dr. Dolan had any notion of the fees he and Roger charged, the better to work less and be choosy about the cases they accepted.

"We don't know that it was a man."

"What do you mean?" His façade cracked as he asked the question.

"It could have been a woman."

Dolan collapsed in relief. Had he expected Phil to say that it could have been a boy? "Will you work for me?"

"Let's just say I'm as interested as you are in finding out who did this."

Roger had located the hammer and had a cheering theory.

"Phil, it couldn't have been dropped there by Chris. It was flung into the snow from some distance. My guess is from a passing vehicle."

"But Chris could have gone into the roadway."

Roger shook his head. "His tracks exclude that. No, someone else threw that hammer where you found it."

Suddenly, what he had brought from Dolan's clinic took on a new importance.

As a matter of routine, Phil had lifted a veneer of snow from the street behind Dolan's parked car that bore the imprint of the physician's tires. Roger came with him when he drove back to the Carter house.

"I can't go back there," Chris's mother had said.

"Of course not. Stay here."

"Can I play with the computer?" Chris asked.

"No. But you can use it."

The tire print of Dolan's car matched tire prints in the driveway of the Carter home, nearly obliterated now because of all the traffic, but clear enough. Phil put the matching samples in the freezer compartment of the Carter refrigerator.

"Are you going back to his office, Phil?"

"Of course," Phil said grimly.

Dolan interrupted a consultation and took Phil

into his office, his manner anxious. His anxiety increased when Phil told him of the discovery of the hammer.

"I was following Chris's tracks when I came upon it."

"I threw it there," Dolan burst out, seeming to surprise himself, but then he repeated it. "I threw it there. I did it, Knight. I killed Carter."

"Why?"

"Why! He took my wife and child. I thought I had accepted losing Marie, but I hadn't. I was overcome by jealousy."

"How did you kill him?"

"With that hammer you found. I threw it there when I drove away." He opened a drawer of his desk removed some gloves, wrapped in a paper towel. "I haven't gotten rid of these yet."

Dolan came docilely to the constable's office and to the sheriff's. A preliminary analysis matched the blood on the gloves and that on the hammer with that of that of the victim. And that was that.

Phil told Roger what had happened, taking his brother to the far end of the house, away from Chris and his mother. Roger followed the account attentively although he couldn't stop moving about on the couch, as if he were seeking an elusive comfort. He began to shake his head.

"It's too neat, Phil."

"It's just neat enough, Roger."

Roger's unwillingness to accept the fact that Dolan's confession closed the case made Phil uneasy. His mountainous brother had a way of making the obvious obscure and vice versa, but all too often his rejection of the obvious led to the solution of the case they were on. Did Roger, despite what he had said about the hammer, think Chris had killed his "new" father? It suddenly dawned on Phil that this was exactly what Dr. Dolan thought. No wonder he had confessed. By taking the blame, he could protect his son.

Roger seemed lost in reverie as he rocked back and forth on the couch. Was he thinking what this would do to the boy psychologically? The fact that Chris had said nothing about what had happened at the Carter house before he fled seemed ominous now. Had he blotted it from his mind?

Roger rocked back and forth and then got himself upright with a gasping sound. Succulent aromas had been drifting to them from the kitchen and now Marie called them to table. Phil supposed he should be grateful for this, but he found himself resenting the woman's helpfulness. Of course she had to get her mind off recent events. Good Lord, had she witnessed Chris's attack on her new husband? And how had the boy managed to run away?

Spaghetti, salad, mountains of garlic bread – a meal that Phil himself might have prepared, but his would never have tasted as good as this. Roger was rosy with contentment, although he had drunk no wine, just a bottle and a half of mineral water. Chris watched in awe as Roger ate and his mother's delight gave way to concern that the food would not be enough. Roger rubbed his face with his napkin.

"Check my e-mail, will you, Chris?"

This was something he had earlier shown the boy how to do. Chris scampered off to the study and Roger looked at Marie over his glasses.

"The hammer has been found, Marie."

"The hammer?"

"It was found beside the tracks Chris made when he came here last night."

She looked from Roger to Phil. "Surely you don't think . . ."

"Your husband was at your house last night, wasn't he? Your first husband?"

"Jeff?" She assumed a look of disbelief. "Why would he have been there?"

Phil intervened, desperate to comfort the distraught woman. "He's already confessed, Marie. And everything bears out the truth of what he says. He was there, he threw away the hammer when he left, he still had the bloody gloves he wore."

"What really happened last night?" Roger asked her. She drew in her breath slowly and then said,

"It wasn't Jeff. I did it. I killed Henry."

Phil smiled indulgently. "And then threw the hammer away from where it was found?"

Her eyes darted from brother to brother. "No. That was Jeff. I called him and told him what I had done. He insisted on coming. He thought that if we made it appear that someone had broken in . . ."

Polk's reaction to the news that Marie had confessed to the murder of Henry Carter was that she and Dolan had done it together. That was when Roger asked to visit the scene of the crime. The constable assured him it had been gone over with a fine tooth comb and he could tell Roger anything he wanted to know right here in his office. But Roger persisted and soon they were on their way to the Carter house, in the van with Polk following reluctantly. He was an unhappy guide as he led them to the unheated porch where the body had been found. Roger stared at the spot of blood on the carpet, blinking and humming.

"Let's look at the rest of the house."

"This is where the body was found," Polk protested.

"Carter didn't die here," Roger said.

"What do you mean?"

Phil convinced Polk to humor Roger and they followed him as he moved slowly through the living room and eased himself through the door of the den. Polk assured him that no one had disturbed this room.

"I've never been in here before."

But Roger had stooped to study a framed diploma that was propped on the leather couch. His eyes lifted to the wall and he began to nod. A moment later he was tugging a towel out from under the couch. It was discolored with dried blood. The carpet had been hastily cleaned, but it too was stained.

"This is where it happened," Roger said. "They must have taken the body from here to the porch."

"They?"

"Marie and Dr. Dolan."

"But why?"

"Why don't we let them tell us that."

Questioned closely, with Mortimer there and Polk's deputy, the two confessed murderers seemed unsure what exactly had happened and their stories constantly conflicted. Mortimer said the body had been dead for hours by the time the 911 call had been made and Polk and Phil took turns questioning the hapless man and woman. Finally Roger held up a hand.

"Marie, was it Chris's absence that made you think he had done it?"

"Chris! No, of course not. I did it."

Dolan insisted that he did. "I turned over the bloody gloves; I threw away the murder weapon."

"But it wasn't a murder weapon," Roger said sweetly and everyone stared at him. "Carter must have been standing on the couch to drive the nail on which to hang that framed diploma. You can see it there, hardly driven into the wall at all. I imagine he lost his balance but kept gripping the hammer because it was the only thing he could get hold of. I suspect that he flailed about and it got behind his head and he fell on it when he struck the floor."

Silence. Marie looked at Roger and then at her former husband. She was trying to see the scene as Roger described it.

"After you found Carter's body, you discovered Chris was missing, didn't you?"

She began to nod, seeing it all now. That was when she had called Dolan and of course he had come immediately. Both father and mother assumed that Chris had killed the new father he hated, and their first and common impulse was to protect their son.

Polk was reluctant to release his prisoner, but eventually Marie and Dolan were at the Knights, reunited with Chris. They seemed appalled that they had imagined their son had actually killed a man. The three sat huddled together on the couch, the fire blazing and Phil mulling wine. Roger took Chris off to the kitchen for hot chocolate. The boy was delighted by the apparent reunion of his parents.

"What was the diploma?" Phil asked later, when everyone had gone and they had the house to themselves again.

"It was a certificate of recognition."

"For what?

"Carter was a blood donor."

"Greater love than this," Roger began, but then his voice faded as he began to doubt the appropriateness of the allusion.

2

Dust Abhors a Vacuum[2]

Aunt Lucerne was the only relative Philip and Roger Knight had, so it was perhaps fitting that she should be absolute. Once in the dimly remembered past she may have entertained doubts, but this was long before her nephews came to know her. In their experience, she had always been omniscient, riddled with certainty and usually wrong. She was at her most Olympian on this visit.

She sat enthroned in a straight and unforgiving chair, to the left of the fireplace in which no fire blazed, this having been forbidden by Aunt Lucerne as unnecessary in April.

"The temperature is 33," Philip said.

"Fahrenheit," Roger added. But it was folly to think that Aunt Lucerne's outlook could be influenced by mere facts. Her rounded eye had turned on Roger and her brows lifted.

2 A Roger Knight Mystery, by Ralph McInerny, *Crisis* Magazine, March 1997

"You're fat."

"Yes, I am," Roger said cheerfully. "I weigh well over three hundred pounds."

"Good Lord."

"Amen."

"No one in our family is fat," she said, sitting even straighter. To say that Aunt Lucerne was slight of build would have been to sin on the side of charity. To be sure, she had with age begun to shrink and melt, in the usual fashion, but some icebergs make it much farther into southern waters than others. What she meant, Roger decided, was that she did not feel fat.

Her attention returned to the mission that had brought her half a thousand miles to the house of her nephews in Rye, New York. She lifted the shopping bag she had been holding since sailing in unannounced fifteen minutes before. Her hands were in need of a fire (and some hot chocolate as well), but she waived away the suggestion.

"The contents of this bag are an insult."

The two brothers waited. She seemed to expect more of a response.

"You are Philip?"

"I am."

"I am told that you are intelligent."

"Word gets out."

"I am also told that you are a detective."

"Yes."

"Good at puzzles, able to understand odd things?"

"Sometimes."

That established, she turned once more to Roger.

"And you are a Catholic?"

"That's right."

That an overweight Catholic should be related to her by blood was clearly a trial for Lucerne. But the question was relevant. She briskly laid out for them the reason for her visit.

The shopping bag contained the contents of a safe deposit box that had been held in the name of her estranged husband. Their marriage had received its final blow when he converted to Catholicism.

"He said he had "poped." I did not know the word. This seemed to give him pleasure. Eventually I caught his meaning. It was the last straw."

"You parted?"

She glared at Roger. "He left." Her tone conjured an image of herself in the doorway, pointing toward the horizon while her disgraced husband skulked off into the sunset. "Since you too have poped," she said, wincing, "I thought that perhaps you might discern some twisted significance in what he has done. Your superstitions plus your brother's brains may make some sense of this." She rattled the shopping bag.

News of her husband's death had reached her only after the fact, not that she meant to suggest that she would have hastened to be at his bedside. "There are some things only God can forgive."

Silence fell. Neither brother was inclined to inquire into the precise nature of their uncle's perfidy. Neither had either of them met the man. Since separating from him, Lucerne herself had neither seen nor talked with her husband, Fergus. When she heard that he had left instructions that a key to a safe deposit box be given to her, Lucerne had felt faint stirrings of the milk of human kindness.

"One reads of deathbed repentance, I imagined this was a case of it. The key arrived. The box was in a bank of the city in which I live. Minneapolis," she added, peering at Philip.

"Minneapolis," he repeated.

"Actually, Edina. A suburb."

"So you went to the bank?"

She ignored Roger. She was not to be hurried through her narrative. She was clearly intent on telling them in such a way that it would be unnecessary to go over painful matters again and again.

Admitted to the vault and eventually left alone with the box that had been removed from its place and put on a table where she might inspect it, she had felt the significance of the moment. A faint tremor passed through her body. Less loathsome memories of her spouse assailed her. Almost, she remembered having some smidgen of affection when she consented to Fergus Tracy's pleas and agreed to become his wife.

The corners of her mouth had dimpled with the promise of a smile and then she lifted the cover of the box.

"It was one final insult, from beyond the grave," she cried, the ignominy of that moment returning in full force.

"What did you find?" Roger asked.

"It is all here. As soon as I recovered, I scooped the contents of the box into this shopping bag lest anyone see what Fergus had dared do to me."

"And you have brought everything to us?" Philip said. His eye was on the shopping bag and Roger recognized a more than professional curiosity in his brother's eye. From time to time they had spoken of Aunt Lucerne but always in a negative vein. After all, she had responded to a Christmas card with a note that they need never again bother to visit such sentimentality on her. Roger continued to send her a card nonetheless. She wrote to tell him that she had little money and that in any case it was already destined to go elsewhere. Reliving their aunt's humiliation in the bank vault when she opened the safe deposit box warmed Phil almost as much as a good fire in the hearth might have.

"Take it," she cried, holding the bag at arm's length.

Philip went for it. Roger was on his feet and at his brother's side when he pulled aside the bag's handles to look inside.

"A cheesehead?" Roger asked.

"And a piggy bank," Philip noted.

"It is empty," Lucerne said with a disdainful and ladylike snort.

Philip removed what Roger had called a cheesehead, a triangular piece of yellow plastic made to look like cheese and worn as hats by fans of the Green Bay Packers. He turned it over, shook it, smelled it, looked at Roger, and surrendered it to him. Roger put it on the table. There seemed nothing distinctive about the unusual headgear: There were doubtless thousands and thousands identical to it.

The piggy bank was a promotion item from a Green Bay bank, a rotund ceramic porker wearing a beatific smile with a slot on its back. On one side was lettered "Mac Livid." On the opposite side was a piece of masking tape on which was lettered, "Your name." The triangular sides of the headgear were blank

"Who is MacLivid?" Philip asked.

"If I knew that I would not be here."

"Have you called this bank?"

She inhaled through her nostrils in a protracted way, seeming to inflate with the activity, her eyes closed as if in pain. "I must have an intermediary. You must see how foolish I would look making such inquiries about an empty piggy bank."

"But there has to be some reason for passing these things on to you."

"Of course there is. He imagined me calling that bank and asking foolish questions, doubtless causing a flood of gossip about the grasping widow. You must do it for me."

"So you are convinced that these things mean something?"

"I am convinced of nothing of the sort. More than likely it is a practical joke, meant to mock me. I will not give Fergus that satisfaction, not even posthumously."

"How long can you stay, Aunt?"

"How long will it take?"

"That is difficult to say."

"But you think you can find out what it means?"

"I can try," Philip replied and there was a barely suppressed chuckle in his tone. Roger feared that his brother would take culpable pleasure in prolonging their Aunt Lucerne's suspense.

"She is torn between two possibilities," Philip said later when Aunt Lucerne had consented to stay with them and had gone up to the guest room.

"Like Buridan's ass," Roger murmured.

"Don't be unkind."

Roger tried to explain the allusion, but Philip was turning over the cheesehead and inspecting the piggy bank, a grin on his face.

"I wish we had known Fergus better, Roger."

"We didn't know him at all."

Philip regarded the point as pedantic. "MacLivid," he said, reading the side of the pig.

"Any idea what it means?"

"Probably nothing. The old girl may be right. It's just his way of getting back at her."

Roger considered the likelihood of such posthumous vindictiveness and ranked it slight. Aunt Lucerne had asked Philip if he was good at solving puzzles and grasping the point of obscure things. She must have known her husband as well as anyone and found it difficult to accept the theory that this was merely a practical joke.

Aunt Lucerne was without comment on the excellent dinner Philip had prepared and afterward remarked that television gave her a headache. She settled down with a book written to help its readers achieve a higher estimate of themselves, a singular waste of time in her case. Roger repaired to his computer and soon was happily in communication with his peers throughout the world. A child prodigy, Roger had received a doctorate from Princeton at the age of 21. It was at Princeton that he had converted to Catholicism. A teaching career failed to open up for him: He was eccentric, putting on more weight daily, and had a childlike innocence that caused people to doubt that he was as brilliant as his dossier suggested. An unemployable genius. He settled down with Philip who, after several muggings, decided he would conduct his private investigation business from the redoubt of Rye, advertising an 800 number in the yellow pages of directories about the country and taking only jobs that promised diversion as well as money. Roger applied for and received a private investigator's license and they had become partners of a sort. Roger was left with considerable leisure to read and carry on exchanges over the Internet with a far-flung circle of electronic pals.

Philip went to Green Bay and made inquiries at the bank that had given out the piggy banks some ten years before. The director fondled the pig as if a prodigal had come home. MacLivid? He knew no one of that name. What did he make of the lettering on the piggy bank's side? He was a stolid man, in Philip's description, a man whose imagination was not given much exercise. With reluctance he let Philip inspect the records of holders of safe deposit boxes. There was none in the name of Fergus Tracy and none in the name of MacLivid.

"Did you try the Mc's as well as the Mac's?" Roger asked on the phone.

"Of course."

Philip returned unsuccessful from his trip to Wisconsin. Aunt Lucerne had trouble controlling her contempt.

"And you call yourself a detective?"

"I think you are withholding information from me."

She fell back in her chair, her mouth agape.

"Withholding information. About those ridiculous items? I know no more about them than you do, apparently. I was right, you see. It is merely a stupid, mean-spirited joke." She whacked her thigh with her self-help book. "I wish I had never come."

She planned to leave the following morning. It was during the night that Roger had his epiphany, whether sleeping or waking he was not sure. But the solution to the riddle Aunt Lucerne had brought suddenly seemed as obvious as could be. He told her this at breakfast.

"I don't want to talk about it."

"Your name means your name."

"What?"

"Lucerne."

"Lucerne means Lucerne?"

"You put Lucerne in the spot covered by the tape saying 'Your name'"

"What on earth for?"

"The cheesehead," Roger said patiently. "It is Swiss cheese."

"Lucerne, Switzerland?" Philip asked. "You think there is someone named MacLivid in Lucerne?"

"I doubt it very much."

"But MacLivid is lettered on the pig."

"Numbered, not lettered. I think he was using Roman numerals.

Mouth still open, Aunt Lucerne looked from one nephew to the other, as if she had fallen among idiots. They were trying to establish the numerical equivalent of MacLivid.

"Forget the 'A' after the initial 'M.' He presumed we would substitute 'Mc.'"

"One thousand one hundred."

"Eleven hundred," Roger agreed. "But it is a jerry-built construction. I think it means 1154499."

"And what does that mean?" Aunt Lucerne said, but she was unable to retain her note of indignation.

"It means that I have to take a long trip," Philip said.

Roger was left to entertain Aunt Lucerne, who wanted him to go over the interpretation of her inheritance again and again. Each time he explained, she shook her head as she listened. "It doesn't make sense."

"It's a riddle."

"Fergus was mean, but he was not capable of anything as complicated as this."

"It's not complicated."

She turned down her mouth, as if she thought Roger were congratulating himself.

"I'll bet your brother will find a Mr. MacLivid."

"You mean Monsieur MacLivid. Or Herr. Maybe even Signore MacLivid."

Aunt Lucerne tuned him out, going back to her

book. Roger had managed a peek at its contents. Its chapter titles suggested a diffidence foreign to Aunt Lucerne. Don't Undersell Yourself. You're Right Until You Say You're Wrong. Ten Tips on How to Win Arguments. Among the ten Roger found: Never concede. Be aggressive. He began to think that his aunt had written the book.

Two days later Philip called long distance from Switzerland. Aunt Lucerne had snatched up the phone.

"What do you mean, Bingo?"

"Roger was right."

"You found a Mr. MacLivid."

"Is Roger there?"

"I'm on the other phone, Phil."

"It was the number of a safe-deposit box, but it was also the name in which the box had been taken out."

"Did they let you see what was in it?"

"No, but they let Mr. MacLivid."

"And we are now talking to him?"

"Aunt Lucerne, are you still on? There was a message with the money."

"A message?"

"'Put this in your piggy bank.' That's the message."

"You say there's money?"

"A great deal of money."

"But how much?"

"Enough to fill a piggy bank."

When Roger came back to the living room, his aunt sat with her hand still on the hung-up telephone, wearing a stunned expression as she stared at the fireless grate. When she became aware of Roger's presence, she turned and looked sharply at him. But then the expression faded and she looked at him almost with fondness.

"Fergus was a good man."

"I hope he didn't steal the money."

This sent her into an extended fit of agitation, but soon she had convinced herself that her dear Fergus would not do anything either unethical or illegal.

She professed to find it endearing that he had made over his money to her in so oblique a manner.

"Well, what good is an empty piggy bank?" Roger asked.

Her eye roved over nephew's expansive self and a cutting remark seemed to form itself on her lips. But she forbore scolding him.

"What good indeed?"

3

The Eye of the Beholder[3]

Mae Brown's house was set back on her lot, on a slight knoll. On the opposite side of the road an imposing hill rose almost mountain-like. At various levels of its elevation there were houses and it was one of Mrs. Brown's innocent pleasures to sit in her front window and look across the road at the inexhaustibly interesting hillside. Not only were some of the houses at a considerable distance from her own but, because they were high on the hill, were as a practical matter even farther off. Not that she ever visited them, of course, though she thought of their occupants as her neighbors and in a sense they were.

The binoculars Roger Knight had given her so that she could keep a closer watch on the neighborhood had been a joke, of course, but she had acquired the habit of using them. It was odd how the same house could look so different viewed with or without the binoculars.

3   A Roger Knight Mystery, by Ralph McInerny, *Crisis* Magazine, April 1997

She knew them not by name of owner but by descriptions taken from what she could see from her front window. There was the house with the Irish setter, another with a metal maintenance shack that reflected the afternoon sun annoyingly back to Mrs. Brown. There was the brick house, the ranch, what she thought of as the bird house and then the barn.

It was no longer a barn, of course, having been converted for occupancy some years back. But it retained the shape and look of a barn and a barn it was to Mae Brown. It was next to the barn that one afternoon she saw something so awful she could scarcely believe her eyes.

A man in a bright plaid jacket came out the door, bent over, leaning forward, dragging something after him. So limp was the burden that it did not occur to Mrs. Brown at first that it was a man. The inert body was pulled to a stump where it was arranged in a kneeling position, the head resting on the table-like surface of the stump. The man in the plaid jacket then returned to the barn. When he emerged again, he was carrying an axe. Mae Brown's mouth had gone dry. For an awful minute the plaid clad arms lifted the axe high and then seemed to freeze. Mae Brown sat staring at the tableau, wanting to turn from her window or pull the drapes but unable to follow this sensible advice.

Suddenly the axe was brought down in a great sweeping arc. The head leapt free of the body and rolled across the lawn. Despite the distance and her weak eyes Mae was certain she not only saw blood but also the way it beaded as it fell. And then came the sound of the axe striking the stump after it had severed the head. Mae cried out, her hand flying to her throat.

Three minutes later nothing remained of what she had seen. The man in the plaid jacket was gone, the stump was gone, and the two pieces of the initially unconscious and now dead man had disappeared. Mae shut her eyes and then let them open.

"That didn't happen," she said aloud.

She went into the kitchen and made a cup of tea. She kept her back to the windows, not wanting to look across the road at the barn. She took the tea into the living room, sat, added sugar and cream and stirred it thoroughly. When she peered across the road at the barn, there was nothing to see.

"It didn't happen," she said again and tried to laugh.

When the telephone rang, Roger ignored it, continuing what he was doing at the computer. The ringing stopped and the voice of his brother Philip drifted to him, and something about Phil's tone was more distracting than a bell. Roger turned in his specially built chair and cocked an ear toward the other room.

"No, Mae, I think you're right. It couldn't have happened."

A silence followed during which Roger thought of Mae Brown, the elderly woman up the road from their place. They felt informally responsible for her, since she lived alone in the house where she had raised her children. Her husband was gone now and the children were far-flung, one in Japan, the other in San Diego.

Mae was forever pondering invitations to come visit, but in the end she decided against it and stayed put.

Visits from her children were infrequent and hurried, although she often talked to them on the phone, particularly Evelyn in San Diego. For the Knight brothers, Mae substituted for the mother they had lost when they were boys and it was pleasant to feel that they were responsible for her.

"Well, at that distance, you could have been easily deceived." A pause. "Even with the glasses."

When Roger had given her the binoculars, he had suggested that she make note of the different birds that came within view of her window, but he knew and she knew that she found it restful just to sit at her window and look out over the road to the hills beyond and the homes scattered along them. Sometimes at night, Roger would look out in the same direction, at the irregular pinpoints of light of varying intensity. It might have been a fallen portion of the night sky. The view, night or day, did have an oddly mesmerizing effect.

"I may take it up myself in my old age, Philip."

"Staring at the computer for hours doesn't make a lot more sense."

"Less. Looking across at those hills is far more contemplative."

He didn't expect Phil to agree. Phil didn't have a contemplative bone in his body. All the more reason to admire his sympathy and compassion with Mae Brown.

"She thinks she saw someone chop off someone else's head."

"What?"

Phil gave him the story in the same detail he would have gotten it from Mae, and Roger felt a little twinge of concern that Mae should think she had seen such a thing. His own limited experience suggested that one's gaze constantly traveled from object to object, seldom lingering for long on one house, tree, vehicle. At night it was even less likely that one would concentrate on one object. It was the whole panorama of light and darkness that held one's desultory attention.

Obviously it was wrong to suggest to Philip that such aimless gazing was contemplative. It seemed rather the essence of harmless distraction.

"She's pretty sure where it happened. There's a reconverted barn and a mobile home . . ."

"I think the barn is new."

"You know the place?" Phil turned toward the window and did not have to search long for the house May described.

"What do you call it when people think they see axe murders?"

"Does it have a name?"

"I hope not."

Mae had survived her husband and lived longer than either of her parents, but this could have its drawbacks. The longer one lived the more ills and ailments he was subject to. And there was always the specter of senility.

Roger shook the thought away. A human life was not just a matter of pleasure and pain. Mae was a

Catholic, like himself, and would have given a crisp catechetical answer to the question of what the meaning of life is. Still, the days grew long and she wearied of television. There was something sad about the image of an old woman staring through the window at the distant scenery. He imagined her nodding off and dreaming an axe murder and then coming awake and thinking she had actually seen it happen.

"She kept saying that of course it didn't really happen."

Phil took comfort in this and went off about his own business while Roger turned back to his computer. He had found a web site where the works of Kant were accessible in the original and he was reacquainting himself with *the Critique of Pure Reason*. What would Kant have made of Mae's report? What we see is what we see, according to the philosopher, what appears, that is, and this is never the same as what really is. The theory accounted for mistakes and even hallucinations, but nonetheless it made all sense experience seem hallucinatory. A theory like Kant's, Roger was convinced, was something only a philosopher could take seriously.

But beating up on dead philosophers had its limitations as an indoor sport, and Roger soon found himself at the front window, with binoculars, looking across the road. The mobile home came into sight and he moved the glasses slowly to the right. The side of the barn seemed to jump up from nowhere, filling his field of vision. He shut his eyes and when he opened them again the focus had dropped and he was looking at a stump.

It was a weather-beaten thing, actually a section of a tree, not something that had grown where it stood. The top looked stained and Roger could not help thinking of Mae's claim of what she had seen. All too easily he imagined the fall of the axe and the head rolling away across the yard. He actually looked for it, through the glasses. He found nothing, of course, but when he tracked back to the barn something came into view that stopped him. An axe was propped against the barn, beside the door and Roger wondered if that was the door that had figured in Mae's hallucination. A man in a plaid coat had emerged from it, dragging his unconscious victim to that stump to lop his head off.

"Just a drive?" Phil said, turning from the television set where a game was in progress.

"For a change. I haven't been out of the house for days."

"So what's new?"

Roger was a homebody, no doubt about it. When he offered to drive himself, Phil scrambled out of the chair, a look of terror forming on his face.

Don't be silly. I'll drive."

"Who's winning?"

"I'm not even sure who's playing."

That, Roger was sure, was a white lie, meant to relive any guilt he might feel for tearing Phil away from the set. It was a moment when he could have changed his mind, gone back to his study, taken a nap. But he waited for Phil and then they went out to the van.

The van had been designed to their specifications, since it was in it that they did all their traveling. Phil did not like to fly, but in Roger's case it was impossible. There was no way he could fit into an ordinary airline seat, neither were those in first class ample enough for him. Jokes about sending him air freight had worn thin. In any case, traveling in the van was something both brothers enjoyed. But its design was not really conducive to just driving around. In the back a special chair had been devised for Roger, one that rotated, enabling him to face any point on the compass. There was an adjustable desk for a portable computer, a cellular phone to accommodate his modem. He did not lose contact with his electronic friends when he and Phil were on the road.

"Where to, Roger?"

"Oh, nowhere in particular."

The verdict on ESP and the transmission of thought was not yet in, but Roger concentrated, hoping Phil would get the idea without any need to say it. They seemed to have agreed not to take Mae Brown's call seriously.

"We could drop in on Mae."

"On the way back?"

"From where?" And then Phil smiled. "Why don't we check out the scene of the axe murder?"

Roger relaxed. It would have been impossible to prove that his thought had had anything to do with Phil's association of ideas. But is everything in our world susceptible of proof?

Phil went to town and ran in for pipe tobacco as if to underscore that the proposed destination was just a lark. Behind the wheel again, he went back to the first intersection and then turned toward the hills, following a county road. Lesser roads led away from it, in both directions, and the one they finally took was quite a bit below the barn. Phil had to continue on for some distance before there was an opportunity to climb higher. They came slowly back and began to catch glimpses of the barn.

"Can you see our place from here, Roger?"

"Not really. I know where it is, but the trees block it."

The people who lived on the hill would not consider themselves to be objects on view for those below. Everything here was where it was, not an object in the distance.

"Here we are," Phil called out. He had come around a turn in the road and there was the barn.

"And there he is, Phil."

A man in a plaid coat was standing by the barn, hands on his hips, staring at it. There was a sign over the door. Hillside Theater. Below it was another legend. *A Man for All Seasons.* Both brothers laughed at the same time and Phil pulled in.

His name was Page; he had the self-absorbed look of an actor and listened with an indulgent smile while Phil told him of Mae Brown's report.

"Yesterday?" His expression became theatrically pensive. "Of course. She did indeed see what she thought she saw."

In the final scene, the execution of Thomas More; they did not, of course, intend actually to execute the actor.

"Tempting as that is," Page said, and his smile lost something of its warmth.

A dummy was substituted for the saint and Page had been testing whether the head would indeed roll free when the rubber axe fell.

"The lights go out immediately. It was tremendously effective."

Another man came out of the barn, paused as if to make certain all eyes were on him and then progressed toward them in a stately manner.

"This is Manchester," Page said icily. "Never out of character. We have guests, Sir Thomas."

Manchester was the actor who played Thomas More in the play and he listened to the story of what an old woman down in the valley had seen, a disapproving smile on his lips, as if the folly of mortals gave him pain. Roger wondered if the actor had any sense of the character he played.

They stopped at Mae's on the way home and it was considerably later than they would have expected. Wandering around the hillside roads was an adventure neither had a desire to repeat. They were still with Mae when the dreadful story appeared on the news. The old woman let out a little cry and clapped a hand over her mouth. Her wide eyes traveled from brother to brother.

"What an incredible coincidence," Phil said, looking to Roger for corroboration. But Roger was following the account of the beheaded body that had been reported at the Hillside Theatre just minutes before.

The first pictures came in and while the cameraman tried to strike a balance between satisfying the viewer's curiosity and arousing disgust, the fallen body in the plaid coat beside the stump was all too reminiscent of Mae's story. A blanket had been thrown over the shoulders. Phil got up and turned off the television.

"No need for you to watch such stuff, Mae."

"I've already seen it," she said in a small voice.

Phil protested but back to the barn theater they went. The investigation was in full flow when they got there and Manchester was center stage.

"Some men came earlier with a story of what someone had seen from down there." His arm lifted, a finger uncurled, stiffened, pointed. "We were enacting the scene."

And then he saw Roger and Philip and called them forward. "These are the men of whom I speak."

The sheriff looked at them with mingled relief and annoyance. It was not an unmixed blessing to have private detectives in a jurisdiction as small and generally peaceful as his own. Manchester repeated the story he had earlier told Page, while Roger wandered to the tragic scene. A minute later Roger came back.

"Arrest him," he advised the sheriff.

Manchester fell back, a splayed hand on his breast. "You haven't been paying attention. We were playing a scene, Page took my place . . ."

"You used a real axe," Roger said. "Surely you can tell the difference between the real and the make-believe?"

Manchester was not so taken aback that he failed to insist that he have a lawyer. Shortly after, for the second time in a few hours, Philip directed the van out of the yard and started homeward.

"It wouldn't have happened if it hadn't been for Mae's story."

"Don't tell her that, Phil."

"I won't have to."

Roger frowned and turned in his swivel chair. Had Mae's report of what had not happened become a cause of its happening? He tried the thought out aloud.

"Say that again, Roger?"

But some things said but once are said too often.

4

Partners and Crime[4]

It was a densely wooded plot of land that lay at the intersection of two country roads, not what one would have thought of as remote, but it was not until late October when the leaves had fallen that the old bus became visible from the road. How many motorists caught a glimpse of it in peripheral vision and did not give it a thought would have been difficult to say. Riders of bicycles were more likely to get a good look at it and that is why the two boys scrambled down the bank, crossed the ditch, and picked their way through the thick stand of now-denuded trees to the bus. The side windows were curtained and they could not see much when they peered through the windshield, prepared though they were for God knew what. When they forced open the door, they came upon the suitcase.

"Have you opened it?" Philip Knight asked the taller boy, Dennis.

4 A Roger Knight Mystery, by Ralph McInerny, *Crisis* Magazine, May 1997

"We couldn't," the pudgy one said.

No wonder. It was a bulging calfskin piece of luggage, strapped and locked, its buckles and locks rusted.

"Why did you bring it here?" Roger Knight asked. He lumbered into the room, having been distracted from his computer. The two boys fell back at this vision of a rumpled three hundred-pound giant whose expression was that of a boy like themselves rather than the censorious adult his question might have suggested.

"It looks valuable," said Pudge.

"It smells," Dennis said.

The piece of luggage did create a minor olfactory sensation in the Knight living room. Roger was circling it now, sniffing, squinting, nodding.

"RCM," he said slowly, making out the initials impressed into the calfskin, their gold all but disappeared. He turned and looked at Philip. "RCM," he repeated.

"What's it mean?" Pudge asked, but when Phil spoke he sounded like someone testing a microphone.

"Ronald Charles Murphy?"

"You know him?" Dennis asked, disappointed.

Phil nodded.

"Who is he?"

Murphy had been the partner of a man who came seeking Philip's help when he failed to interest the prosecutor in his partner's alleged peculation. Roger had advised Phil not to take the case even though it was local and would not have required one of their periodic transcontinental migrations.

It has the look of a domestic quarrel," Roger said.

Philip did not take divorce cases and Roger was touching on one of his reasons. A client is not grateful to the lawyer who must malign a spouse in order to dissolve a union, however much he or she may urge him on. Phil had thought Roger's fear fanciful in the case of Murphy and Schwartz. They were investment counselors with a small but affluent clientele, complementing one another perfectly. Murphy had the affability of a salesman and Schwartz had the gravitas of a banker. Neither man had done as well alone before the formation of their partnership. Yet each thought the other a drag on his future. Schwartz accused Murphy of diverting assets, squirreling away stock certificates and bonds.

"What did the police say?" Phil asked.

"They wanted to examine the books first!"

"Well?"

Schwartz was indignant. "Ours is a confidential business. I can't have people nosing around in our records."

"You want the prosecutor just to take your word that Murphy is a thief?"

"Murphy got to him first. That was the trouble."

"Murphy complained of you to the prosecutor?"

"He's crazy."

Phil soon realized that he had been crazy to take Schwartz as a client. With Roger's help he managed their own portfolio and he had foolishly thought that he might pick up some valuable knowledge in the course of working for Schwartz. A week after Schwartz had first come to him, he called Phil.

"Come get me out of here," Schwartz said without prelude.

"Where are you?"

"In jail."

"What for?"

"I shot Murphy."

The wound was not fatal, but an over-bandaged Murphy was featured on local television. He was said to have survived an assassination plot. The prosecutor brought a charge of attempted murder against Schwartz.

I should have practiced," Schwartz said.

"Thank God you didn't kill him"

"Alive, he'll be free while I am in jail."

"You won't be in that long."

"He could clean me out in a week. He's already confiscated a third of our assets."

Meanwhile, from his bed of pain, Murphy was telling the sympathetic media that the partner who had shot him had been looting their firm, which had been the cause of the quarrel. Could Murphy prove it? Prove it? Of course he would prove it. He was hiring an independent auditor and wanted the prosecutor to monitor the procedure.

"They should lock him up and throw away the key," Murphy roared.

Schwartz was tried and convicted, but his sentence made it all but certain that he would be paroled after serving a year. No sooner was he in his cell than the audit Murphy had ordered was publicized. There was no doubt that assets were missing from the firm. What was lacking, however, was any proof that Schwartz rather than Murphy was responsible. Dahlheimer, Murphy and Schwartz's accountant, a narrow-faced man with a surprised expression, just looked at the reporter who asked him which partner he thought was guilty. The auditor likewise refused to be drawn into that guessing game. Roland the prosecutor said the matter was under review.

A year had passed, the leaves had fallen, and the valise was discovered by the two boys. At the state prison, Schwartz, who had been a model prisoner, was meeting with the parole board. They decided that he was ready to rejoin society. And the Knight brothers were in possession of a calfskin valise bearing the initials RCM. Having rewarded the boys and gained their promise of silence, at least for now, Philip and Roger went to work on the valise. Not even liberal lubrication with machine oil made the locks and buckles tractable, so Phil had recourse to an ice pick and some garden shears and the valise fell open like a much-read book. As it did so, certificates, bonds, CDs, and cash money issued from it as from a cornucopia. Clearly they were looking at the assets missing from Murphy & Schwartz.

"I'll call the prosecutor," Phil said.

"Why?"

"This is stolen property."

"There is no way to tell that. Can a person steal from himself?"

"A partner can steal from a partnership?

"But which partner?"

"Whose initials are on the valise?"

"What does that prove?"

"That the valise belongs to Murphy.'"

"You think he put all these things into a valise and put it into an abandoned bus where anyone might find it?"

"The chances were one in a thousand those kids would look into that bus."

"If you had stolen this much, would you take that kind of a chance?"

"If you're asking me whether people who commit crimes do stupid things, the answer is yes."

"In that case, Schwartz should soon show up at that abandoned bus to claim his ill-gotten gains."

Phil seized on the idea. Of course. A thief who had stashed away his loot would be back for it. Think of Treasure Island. He talked with Roland the prosecutor, who liked the idea too. They would stake out the bus. They would install cameras to record the scene. They would catch the criminal in the act of reclaiming his stolen goods. Roger having given birth to the idea, lost interest in it, and was preoccupied when Phil reported on the trap that Roland was setting.

"Have you told Murphy of the cameras?"

"No! I want this to be a surprise."

Whether the intramural thief was Murphy or Schwartz would thus be settled by which of them went to the bus to claim the calfskin valise.

"It'll be Schwartz," Phil predicted.

"Why?"

"If it were Murphy, he wouldn't have waited."

"He might have gone to the bus and found the valise was missing."

Phil discounted this. The boys had been the first on the scene for months, as an inspection of the area around proved. Theirs were the only signs of human visitors. Now snow had begun to fall and it was an easy matter to see that no one had since visited the bus.

"And I don't think Schwartz will wait long. All that time in prison he had to wonder whether the valise was safe."

The cameras at the scene conveyed it to monitors in the Knights' house, which was not too far distant. It was there that Phil and Roland took up their vigil.

"I'll keep in touch," Roger said, slipping into his jacket.

"Where are you going?"

"Into town."

"You're going to drive yourself?" Phil was clearly alarmed.

"I've got a license."

"Of course you've got a license." Phil paused studying his brother. "Roger, this is your showdown as much as anyone's. Stay here with us."

"I won't be long."

"Where can I reach you?"

"The phone in the van."

"You're going to be in the van all the time?"

Roger nodded and stepped into the wintry afternoon. Phil watched his brother go out to the garage, picking his way down the path. His hand went to the door, as if he would go after him, but he stayed inside.

"What's the matter? Roland said. He was seated in comfort before the bank of monitors, a beer in hand, a platter of man-sized sandwiches in front of him.

Roger had made the snack before he left and Phil looked at the sandwiches ruefully.

"He must be mad."

"Angry or nuts?"

"Hey."

"I meant, why miss out on the grand finale?"

Roger was not given to moods, but Phil couldn't help but think that the presence of Roland had robbed Roger of the sense that he and Phil were together on this matter. He began to resent Roland a bit himself. But that was silly. Once the monitors showed what they were waiting for, the prosecutor could put the police in action with a phone call.

An hour and a half later the sandwiches were gone and Roland was on his third beer and their watch on the monitors was less vigilant. Phil had called the van several times but gotten no answer.

"Look!" Roland cried suddenly in a stage whisper.

There was action on two monitors and at first Phil thought it was two shots of the same man, but then he saw they were different.

"Schwartz," Roland said.

"Murphy," Phil said.

The two men came gingerly through the snow, concentrating on their footing, unaware of one another. A camera mounted high in a tree now gave an aerial view. Murphy and Schwartz were vectoring toward the bus, coming from opposite directions, shielded from one another by the intervening vehicle. Roland and Phil sat forward. This was more drama than they had counted on. And confusing. Why were both men creeping up on the vehicle in which the calf-skin valise of stolen stocks and bonds had been hidden?

Murphy had arrived at the entry door to the bus, but before he could push it open, Schwartz came around the front of the bus. Murphy was visibly startled by the appearance of his partner and on Schwartz's face appeared a look of triumph. The two men rushed at one another, slipping and sliding in the snow and then they were grappling. By the time Roland was putting through his call to the patrol cars that were waiting to descend on the scene, the partners were wrestling in the snow.

Half an hour later, the two partners were in the Knights' living room, where a hefty officer made sure they could not resume their fight. Since there was no cause for arrest it seemed best to take them where they could see the monitors and the vigil that had been kept, waiting for them to make a move.

"I got a call telling me to look in that bus."

"Ha. I got the call. I can't believe I didn't recognize your voice." Murphy sneered at Schwartz and was answered in kind.

"You both got calls?"

"I got a call," the partners said in unison.

And so it went on for some minutes, each accusing the other. They were still at it when Roger returned. He had brought Dahlheimer with him and the accountant seemed reluctant to witness the plight in which his employers had fallen.

"What did you expect to find in the bus?" Roger asked the partners.

"What he stole," was their single answer.

"Just lying in the bus. In a sack? In a box? What?"

Schwartz had no answer and neither did Murphy.

"They're both innocent," Roger said firmly.

Roland said that they couldn't be. There were the missing stocks and bonds.

"Indeed there are. And the one who called knew that they were in the bus."

He knew all right," Murphy said, pointing at Schwartz who was pointing at him.

"Stop him would you, Phil?"

Dahlheimer had started for the door and he broke into a run when Roger spoke. But Phil was too fast for the accountant. Murphy and Schwartz watched all this in amazement.

"Dahlheimer is the embezzler," Roger said. "By causing dissension between the partners he covered his own trail."

"That's a lie," the accountant squealed.

"It was you on the phone," Murphy said. Schwartz was nodding.

"I should have recognized him."

"He tried to disguise his voice."

The two partners looked at one another. More than a mutual recrimination dissipated as they moved toward one another, arms spread and then they were embracing, patting one another on the back, uttering the inarticulate monosyllables with which the male expresses what cannot be said.

"What put you onto Dahlheimer?" Phil asked later. They were at table, savoring huge helpings of Roger's goulash.

"Elimination. If both partners were telling the truth, there had to be someone else. And there was. They were so busy accusing one another they overlooked the one person who could have stolen from them both."

Murphy seemed as happy to get back his valise as what was in it.

"Sentiment always trumps money," Roger observed.

Phil thought about that. It was a nice thought, though he doubted it was always true. Isn't greed a sentiment? No need to discuss it now, however, not with a mountain of goulash before him.

5

Dead Language[5]

An hour after arrival in Minneapolis, Philip Knight called on his client, but the man who answered the door was clearly a policeman.

"Is Genevieve Magee at home?"

"Who are you?"

Though he was on a step below the man, Philip could see the top of his head.

"I was going to ask you the same thing."

"Detective Fleischer."

"City?"

Fleischer nodded. "What's your business?"

"I'm a private investigator."

"Come to se Genevieve Magee?"

"That's right."

"She's dead."

Roger had taken the call three days earlier and

5 A Roger Knight Mystery, by Ralph McInerny, *Crisis* Magazine, June 1997

when he found that the prospective client was a classicist, he spoke to her for forty-five minutes about Tacitus before getting to the point of her call. Of course theirs was an 800 number, so this was not a hardship to Miss Magee, who felt her life was threatened and was inquiring about receiving protection from Knight Investigations.

"I particularly like the connotations of Knight."

"Who would threaten you?"

"I am an heiress."

"It must be a considerable sum."

"Not quite $40 million, I'm told."

The combination of Tacitus and that amount of money was irresistible, and the following morning Philip and Roger rolled down their driveway in their van and started for Minneapolis.

"I should have flown," Philip lamented when he found his client was dead.

"You still would have been too late."

Genevieve had called Monday afternoon at five, which was four o'clock in Minneapolis. The estimated time of death was five o'clock local time. It had been a quiet death. The strong sedative in her tea had put her to sleep and then a pillow had been held over her nose and mouth until life departed her body. She was found slumped in her wheelchair, the pillow on the floor beside her, the overturned cup of tea on the little reading desk attached to her chair. Roger studied the black and white photographs that Fleischer provided.

"The picture seems almost posed."

"She lived with her aunt, Mrs. Owens, the one who intended to bequeath her the money."

Alma Owens did not have the look of a wealthy woman. She wore slacks, ankle-high shoes, and an unbuttoned lumberjack shirt over a T-shirt that bore the legend BULL. Roger asked if she supported only one member of the Chicago NBA team. After a delay, she laughed.

"You should see what's on the back."

"Tell us what happened."

"Is it true that my niece hired you to come protect her?"

"She said she was in danger."

"Well, I want to hire you to find out who did this."

"We intend to do that in any case," Philip said. "As a matter of honor. But we'll be glad to have you for a client. Have you any idea who could have done this?"

Alma Owens mixed mild profanity with a surprisingly extensive vocabulary. She was, it soon emerged, the Alma Owens whose study of the use of Latin in the American colonies and by the founders of the nation was a favorite of Roger's. She had taught her niece Latin and it had been a pleasure of what she refused to call her declining years ("nor conjugating either," she added rolling an eye at Philip) to talk about the classics with Genevieve.

"I found her fascinating on Tacitus."

"He was a surprising favorite of hers."

"Why surprising?"

"Have you read him"

"Of course."

She shrugged. "*De gustibus non disputandum est.*"

There was a third person who lived in the main

house, a diminutive woman who cooked and kept the place clean and had an apartment on the third floor. There was another apartment over the massive garage, originally meant as servants' quarters, and in it lived Sylvia Roche and her husband, Wayne.

"Genevieve's half-sister. And no, the other half isn't a brother." Alma dug Phil in the ribs, apparently convinced he was a roué who regarded the difference in their ages as a mere bagatelle and might shortly declare his intentions.

"What does Wayne do?"

"He works for me, more or less. He's on the payroll anyway. I no longer like to drive and he's a great help to me in that respect."

"And Sylvia?"

Alma Owens sighed. "A saint. Absolutely devoted to Genevieve. And self-effacing. I have begged her to move into the house. The garage apartment does not heat well in winter, and in summer you have to have window air-conditioners going day and night. But she insists it is more than good enough for her and Wayne."

"Is she also your heir?"

Alma pulled her chair closer and whispered. "She doesn't know that. I had decided that everything will be divided between them, with the proviso that Sylvia would take care of Genevieve as long as . . ." She stopped, as if aware for the first time that the grim terminus implied had already been reached.

"So Sylvia would have no motive?"

"For what?"

"To kill Genevieve."

Alma shook her head slowly. "If you had ever seen the two of them together, you would never ask such a question."

That seemed to leave only Mrs. Hopkins, the cook, and Wayne Roche. Roger said he would speak with Roche. A car had been backed out of the garage and parked on the apron, where Roche was engaged in eliciting a high polish from its surface. Roger told him who he was.

"Your aunt has hired us to find out what happened to Genevieve." Roche stared at Roger and suddenly burst into tears. It was a sight to behold: that stocky man whose crew cut made him seem both more youthful and more athletic, crying like a child.

"I'm trying to keep busy, to keep my mind off it. She was a wonderful woman."

"Where's Mrs. Roche?"

"I'd rather you didn't disturb her yet," Roche said and a sob escaped him. "She has taken a sleeping pill."

"What do you do here exactly?"

"Mainly I'm just on call. And of course they need a man around, Aunt Alma and Gen." He began to rub vigorously on the hood of the car.

"Who could have done this to her?"

Roche observed a long significant silence. "It had to be someone in the house."

"Surely not Alma."

"Good Lord, no."

"When do you suppose your wife will awake?"

"I want her to sleep right on through until morning."

Back in the house. Roger settled onto a leather sofa in the library, his lap full of books he had taken from the shelves. His own collection of Latin poets and historians had been purchased haphazardly over the years. It was not until he arrived at Princeton that he studied either Latin or Greek. Prior to that his size and manner had led teachers to think of him as all but retarded. He had been kept two years in the sixth grade but shortly thereafter when Philip, knowing something of his brother's gifts, protested and Roger was adequately tested, everything changed. Roger entered Princeton a year later. He was twenty-one when he took his doctorate in philosophy but the classic languages had remained an abiding love, useful for reading Cicero and Plato and Aristotle, but continuing to seem more a medium for poetry and history than philosophy. Tacitus's *De Germania* had figured in his dissertation, tangentially, and he had looked forward to chatting about that work with Genevieve. It was a poor second best to have access to her books and to those of Alma Owens.

"Most of these works are on the web now," he said to Alma.

She stared at him.

"The Internet."

"I haven't the least idea what you are talking about."

He began to explain it to her, but was interrupted by the arrival of Philip, who immediately saw that Roger was once again assuming that anyone who shared one of his enthusiasms must share them all.

"How long has Mrs. Hopkins worked for you?"

"I consider her one of the family, not an employee."

"Is she in your will too?"

Alma turned to Roger. "You're a nosy one, aren't you?"

"I'm an investigator."

She conceded the point. Yes, Mrs. Hopkins was in the will.

"So it isn't quite accurate to say that you are dividing your estate between Genevieve and Sylvia."

"Shhhh," Alma said. "Sylvia will get it all now, not just half, though she didn't know that."

"She gets all that Mrs. Hopkins doesn't get?"

"Oh, that's not very much at all."

By this she meant five hundred thousand dollars.

"Where did you get all your money?"

"You mustn't laugh."

Roger and Philip promised not to laugh.

"Powerball."

Roger looked blankly at Philip.

"The lottery," she explained. The prize had risen to over $100 million and Alma, a classics professor of modest means, had bought a dollar ticket. And won. "I have never been able to take money seriously since."

This house she had bought and the enlargement of her library were the most obvious results of her good fortune. She had retired from teaching reluctantly, but it was no longer possible to treat and be treated by her colleagues as before. She had once been an esteemed professor, but for all that, like the rest of mortals, now she was a woman of undreamed of wealth.

"People think it confers competency. It does not. I

am told that I can go wherever I wish, and that is true, but do it half a dozen times and it palls. One longs for simplicity. I never fly first class."

"I never fly at all," Roger said.

"I am not surprised. On the other hand if they can lift those massive machines into thin air, I shouldn't think you would pose an insuperable problem."

"It's the seats."

"Ah. Well, there are lots of sofas in this house."

Those in the library were particularly comfortable. Alma told them that one unequivocal benefit of her windfall was her cousin's children had contacted her.

"Genevieve and Sylvia?"

"I remembered mention of a cousin in Omaha, or at least relatives of some kind. But I was left orphaned, if losing both one's parents at thirty-two can be said to make you an orphan, and so had no one I could ask about relatives, distant or close."

"How did you locate them?"

"Oh, they located me."

Mrs. Hopkins, on the other hand, antedated the lucky lottery ticket. "She has known me poor as well as rich."

"How did you know the girls were related to you?"

"A marvelous thing. I'd had my genealogy traced scarcely a month before Sylvia telephoned from Omaha. I found her name and urged her to come as soon as possible. They were the real prize I won."

She handed Roger the results of the genealogical search and he settled down with it. Phil began to talk of what he had learned from Mrs. Hopkins. Some minutes later, Roger looked pensively at Alma.

"I'm surprised someone hasn't tried to kill you."

"Me!"

"Perhaps you don't take money seriously any more, but most people do. Particularly those who stand to inherit a lot of it."

"Well, that was no reason to kill poor Genevieve. I wonder how long she would have lived, with her handicap and all."

"Was she born handicapped?"

"Good heavens no. She was agile as a colt when she first arrived. There was a freak accident. Genevieve had just come in the driveway on her bicycle as the car was being backed out of the garage. The car barely touched her, it seemed, but she was never to walk again."

"Who was her doctor?"

"Sylvia would know. People think I'm tough, but I am simply no good at things like that, other people's pain."

"Who was driving the car?"

"Mrs. Hopkins."

When they were alone, Philip asked Roger what he made of it all.

"I'd like to know how the coroner described Genevieve's physical condition."

"You think the useless legs were a pretense?"

"I don't think anything of the kind. What basis would I have?"

"I'll ask Fleischer."

"Good."

Meanwhile Roger opened his portable computer and got on the Internet, communicating with his far-flung circle of electronic friends. He was especially eager to talk with those who were knowledgeable in genealogies.

"Mrs. Hopkins was right," Philip said some hours late.

"How so?"

"She doubted Genevieve was crippled at all. She swore the car didn't really hit her. Her bike tipped over and she sprawled on the grass but that was it. The coroner said he hadn't noticed anything wrong with her legs."

"Wasn't he curious about the wheelchair?"

"Roche said something that made him think it belonged to Alma."

"I don't think they are even related to Alma, Phil. From what I've been able to learn, this is a bogus genealogy, probably prepared to their specifications. Guess who used to make a living preparing flattering genealogies?"

"One of the girls?"

"Roche."

Phil fell silent "I like her but I can't be guided by that."

"Alma?"

"Mrs. Hopkins. She told me she daydreamed about getting that trio out of here. But she didn't say anything because Alma was so happy to have relatives."

"I'd like to talk to her."

Roger was still in the study when there was the sound of voices in the next room, Phil's and a woman's. And then the door opened and Phil showed in Mrs. Hopkins.

"I'll leave you two alone," Phil said.

"What's this all about?" she asked, frowning at the closing door.

"We work as a team. We're brothers, you know."

"I wouldn't if you hadn't told me. It's not healthy carrying all that weight." Roger peered at her. There was no mistaking the voice.

Roger told her of the embarrassment he had felt when Roche burst into tears. "*Feminis lamentare honestum est,*" he began.

"No, no, no. *Feminis lugere honestum est, viris meminisse.* It is right for women to mourn and for men to remember. You're not very good in the remembering department."

"I remember your voice very well, Mrs. Hopkins. It was you who called and asked us to come here."

"Why on earth would you say that?"

"Because of our interesting chat about Tacitus's *Germania.* Because when I cited what is arguably the only well-turned phrase in the work, you corrected me as you did just then."

She seemed relieved to have been discovered. She sat and was eager to tell him the circumstances of her call. She had just found Genevieve dead in the wheelchair.

"I knew it was the other two. I also knew if I said so Alma wouldn't believe me. She wanted those scoundrels to be her relatives. I thought if you and your brother came and looked into matters . . ."

The staged accident when Genevieve pretended to have been struck by Mrs. Hopkin's car and borrowing the wheelchair Alma had used after a skiing accident

{61{

was meant to turn Alma Owens against her old friend, Mrs. Hopkins.

"That didn't work. I think they hoped I would be suspected of Genevieve's death."

Within minutes, Roger had turned the conversation back to Tacitus. They were on the Agricola when Phil came in with Detective Fleischer. The coroner had found nothing wrong with Genevieve's legs and a wire from Omaha provided grounds enough to arrest the Roches. Alma was brought in and told the whole story. She was dazed and disappointed. But eventually sheepish. She had been blinded by a desire for blood relatives.

"Thank God for Mrs. Hopkins," Roger said. "You can discuss the classics with her."

That Mrs. Hopkins was as knowledgeable as she was came as a surprise to Alma Owens. Apparently Hopkins had been studying Latin for years, having seen what a consolation the classics were to Alma after her bewildering good luck in the lottery.

"Money," Alma said disdainfully. "It is the *radix malorum*."

Mrs. Hopkins and Roger nodded in agreement. Phil and Fleischer shrugged.

6

Fetch

There had been brief stretches of warmer weather, but for the most part the cabin had been marooned in a sea of snow and ice until late April, when the thaw began. Private planes had long since ceased waggling their wings as they flew over, there being no smoke rising from the chimney or other sign of occupation. It was not until May that a canoe was pulled ashore and a camp made and the visitors, presuming on the genial communism of the far north, went to the wood-pile behind the cabin for firewood. A powerful odor nearly drove them back, but then a dread curiosity conquered and the bodies were discovered.

Philip and Roger Knight were about to leave Duluth where Phil had been on a case that was far less interesting than he had expected when Roger heard on the radio of the scene at the cabin. The story was garbled. There were two bodies in the cabin, each had

6 A Roger Knight Mystery, by Ralph McInerny, *Crisis* Magazine, July/August 1997

died from gunshot and then had fallen forward, their heads only inches apart.

"Cabin fever," Phil said. He had some intimation of how trying an otherwise genial person could be from living with Roger in their place in Rye, New York.

"You think it was an argument?"

"I can see it, Roger. They disagree, tempers mount, threats are made, both fire almost at the same time. I wouldn't be surprised if there are playing cards scattered about."

"One was a man, the other a woman."

"A suicide pact," Phil said. The stay in Duluth had dulled his edge and he seemed to think all things were cut and dried.

"No guns were found."

"And both were shot?"

"There was another body too."

"Ah."

"A dog."

"A dog!"

Thus far it seemed an almost algebraic problem. Two bodies found in a remote north woods cabin, both shot, the door locked with a dead bolt lock. The dog had starved to death, its fate perhaps softened by the intense cold that must have penetrated the cabin. Hypothermia would have eased it from this world.

"If the door was locked, Roger, something more than man's best friend was involved. How could he have left?"

"The dog? Oh, there was a flap in the door."

The scene of the crime, if that is what it was, was on their way home – if they took a detour north for several hundred miles. Roger did not chide his brother for his curiosity, though it did seem a bit of a busman's holiday for a private detective. Phil had given up his Manhattan office when he grew weary of being mugged and now worked out of the virtual space of a web page that Roger had set up for him. He could also be reached more conventionally through the 800 number he advertised in the Yellow Pages of several major cities across the nation. Only the intrinsic interest of a case, or an unusually large compensation, could entice him to work. The trip to Duluth did not qualify in the latter sense and Phil's judgment that it did in the former sense had been disproved. Perhaps it was this that whetted his desire to have a look at the cabin in the woods where two people had lost their lives to violence, perhaps mutually administered, though the weapons had yet to be found.

As soon as Sheriff Omar was sure they were not journalists, he was surprisingly forthcoming, but then it must get lonesome for him in this remote town.

"What we usually get is hunting accidents. Or some old duffer strains his heart and dies in a duck blind. Never had a murder before, let alone two."

The couple had been married, although not to one another. Their intention to erase past commitments and marry had been vetoed by Veronica Fielding, the wife of the dead man. The Fieldings, were local, but the other victim, Susan Wambach, had been visiting from Minneapolis when fate, in the form of Art Fielding, struck. He was a shy outdoors type, new in her experience, possessed of a natural gallantry that had won her heart, which was already wandering from

the bland and blasé existence she lived with her husband, Andre, in Edina. The proprietor of Andre's
Restaurant in Minneapolis, Susan's husband had not
yet come north to claim the body of his late wife.

"Said they were as good as split up anyway," the
sheriff said, "I guess if she's kept this long, she can
keep a few more days."

"Still no sign of the weapons?"

Omar shook his head. "I been over that whole lot
myself, from the woods to the shore and from fence to
fence. The only thing I found was a shoe."

He waited for their reaction but the Knight brothers recognized a storyteller when they met one. They
let Sheriff Omar establish his own pace. It turned out
that he had an explanation.'

" Rule out suicide," he said.

"On what basis?"

"They wanted to live together, not die together."

"And that leaves murder?"

"Veronica Fielding found out about her husband
and the lady from the big city and she was on the
warpath. She threatened to kill him if he tried to leave
her."

"She was heard to say that to him?"

"More than once. And she said the same thing to
friends."

"Well, she had motive," Phil conceded.

"But how did she do it?"

"That's the problem."

When her husband and Susan Wambach had disappeared, Virginia took it better than anyone expected. She cried a lot and she wanted the sheriff to

arrange for her runaway husband to be arrested, but she had no idea where he had gone, and anyway, what was the charge supposed to be?

"And all along he was lying out in that cabin dead?"

"We got our first blizzard the day before they disappeared and when winter comes up here it means it. I'm told they could have been dead for months, but they would have been stiff as logs in that unheated cabin. It was the thaw that . . ." His voice trailed away.

"What kind of a shoe?" Roger asked.

"Phil and the sheriff looked at him with alarm.

"The shoe you found when you searched the property."

"Funny thing," the sheriff said, and fell silent. This time Phil rose to the bait.

"How so?"

"It wasn't one of Art's shoes."

"He was wearing two shoes?"

The sheriff nodded. He had put Veronica Fielding under what he called house arrest, meaning that he was counting on her not leaving town while he tried to figure out what had happened to her husband. He assured Phil that if he had the weapon he would arrest her in a minute.

"I don't care what her neighbors would say."

"People backing her up?"

"She's a brand-new widow, an abandoned wife. And rich. Every eligible bachelor for miles around is going to want to console her."

"Anyone in particular?"

Omar looked wise. "Could be."

Veronica Fielding stood up when Roger managed to get through the door sideways and collapse on the center cushion of the sofa, turning it into an easy chair. Phil explained to her who they were.

"You're a private detective?"

"That's right."

"You investigate things?"

Phil said he did.

"I want to hire you. That idiot sheriff doesn't know his chin from his ear lobe. I want you to find out what happened out at that cabin."

The cabin had belonged to them both but Art used it more than she did. Cooking in that primitive kitchen was not her idea of time off. "Plus I don't like to fish."

"How about hunting?"

"I love it. But I don't want to have to cook what I shoot."

"Was the dog a hunting dog?"

"Fetch?" She laughed almost cheerfully. "He was the dumbest dog God ever made. Couldn't be trained. When you tried, he got everything wrong. That's why we called him Fetch. If you threw something and told him to fetch it, he'd pick it up and run away and hide it."

"But he was loyal?"

"Dumb loyal. He could have left the cabin; he could have found his way home . . ."

There was affection in her voice for the dog she had described as dumb. She did not seem a woman who could have killed her husband and his lover, at least not while she was talking of Fetch. But when Phil asked about Susan, a cloud formed on Veronica Fielding's face.

"A Christian should forgive and forget, now that they're dead. But I have Old Testament thoughts about the two of them. I thank God for wreaking vengeance for me. My enemies have been laid low. I would be lying if I said I regretted it."

"Weren't you surprised to find they had been out there in the cabin all along?"

"They left no trail. They could have gone anywhere."

"If you want me to find out who killed them . . ."

"That is merely to clear my name, you understand. So long as the killer runs free there will be people in this town who think I did it."

"Did you?"

She turned to face Roger. "No."

"You were snowbound when they left town?"

"Yes. Can I prove it? I can prove I called the wrecker on my cellular phone and it was nearly fifteen hours before he could get through to me. Of course I could have been to the cabin first and then run off the road."

"Do people think that?"

"They will. I am now a very wealthy widow."

"But that wouldn't have been your motive."

She shook her head. "No, but it's frosting on the cake."

When Roger suggested they check out the cabin and search the property, Phil was not enthusiastic. The sheriff had already done that; the crime scene had been trekked through by too many people to deliver up anything new. Phil wanted to follow the lead Veronica had given him. A man who had owned the lake-shore cabin until he went bankrupt had tried to buy it back, but Art refused. Over time, double the value of the place had been offered and Art's continued refusal had infuriated the man.

"What's his name?"

"Omar."

"The sheriff?"

"His brother Emil."

Of course this intrigued Phil. Roger found it fascinating too, but he was anxious to see the cabin where these strange events had taken place. On the drive out, Phil thought aloud about the way the sheriff had directed their attention to Veronica. "He might have mentioned his brother."

"Brothers look out for one another."

"Yeah."

At the cabin, Phil went inside but Roger began to wander around the property, from time to time stopping and looking out at the lake or back at the cabin. A half-hour later he was down at the boat dock. Before going onto it, he checked out its construction The pistols lay beneath the dock where it ran several feet over the shore.

"Now who do you suppose put those there?" Phil asked. "Whoever it was killed those two, left them in the cabin, locked it, and stashed the pistols out here."

"Why?"

"It could have been her, Veronica, but it might have been the sheriff's brother."

"Why?"

"I heard you the first time. I don't have an answer. I don't know why someone would lock two dead bodies in a cabin for that matter."

"Fetch," Roger said.

"What?"

"I think it must have been Fetch. There was no reason for the killer to hide the weapons. Quite the opposite. Two pistols were used and the bodies arranged in such a way that suicide would be suspected. But the guns were supposed to be found beside the bodies."

"You think a dog hid those pistols under the dock?"

"There are things all around the yard, Phil. I'll bet Veronica will identify them as from the cabin. Maybe it was Fetch's way to try and get the attention of his dead master."

They drove to the sheriff's where Phil intended to ask Omar about his brother. They found a short man with a barrel chest wearing a camel hair coat pacing the sheriff's office. This was Andre Wambach, finally arrived from Minneapolis. He looked ready to turn right around and go home as soon as he took care of things.

"Veronica says she's your client," the sheriff said petulantly.

"She told me about your brother."

"I've got three brothers."

"The one who wanted to buy that cabin back."

"He always liked the place."

"Enough to get rid of an owner who wouldn't sell?"

"Now wait a minute."

"Those are nice shoes," Roger said, and suddenly had everyone's attention. Wambach had stopped pacing and looked down at his shoes.

"Italian made."

"What size are they?"

Andre lifted a brow. "Eight and a half. Why?"

"Do you still have that shoe you found on the property, sheriff?"

"Hey, what is this? Who are these men, sheriff?"

"Just try it on," Roger said.

"What for?"

"So you can clear yourself."

"Clear myself of what?"

"Of killing your wife and Art Fielding."

Andre's mouth dropped open, he spread his arms, his eyes sought the ceiling and the judge above. He was the picture of guilt. Omar had found the shoe and handed it to Roger. Roger lumbered over to Andre and stood before him, an intimidating presence, though he spoke gently. "This is your shoe, isn't it?"

Andre headed for a chair and dropped into it. His eyes traveled around the room. "I should have stayed in Minneapolis."

"This trip?"

He shook his head. "No. Before. I came up here to tell her to get a divorce, cut the comedy, get it over with. I was told they were at the cabin, so I went out there."

"Who told you that?"

"I called Mrs. Fielding."

"You went out to the cabin."

"I did. We talked and she agreed. He just sat there, silent. I wasn't even mad at him. It wasn't his fault she never grew up."

"How did your shoe end up in the yard?"

"Did it? That damned dog went crazy when I started to leave. Art yelled at him, Susan yelled at him. I yelled at him, but he just kept barking and wouldn't let me near the door. Finally, I took off my shoe and threw it at him. I got out the door while he went for it, and headed back to Minneapolis. I was chased halfway home by that blizzard but I managed to keep ahead of it."

Phil shook his head. Sheriff Omar shook his head. "You were there, you had motive, you had opportunity."

"What are you saying?"

"I think you killed your wife and Art."

Andre tried to laugh, but found it difficult since the sheriff was obviously serious.

"Sheriff, I wanted to get rid of her, but not that way. She had agreed to get a divorce. I had accomplished what I came for."

"I have only your word for that."

"Let me call my lawyer."

"Go ahead."

But he was going to have to wait. Roger had the phone. He carefully punched numbers and then waited with closed eyes with the phone pressed to his ears. Then his eyes opened. "Emil?"

The sheriff stood and reached for the phone. "Who you calling?

"I dialed Veronica, sheriff. I got your brother. Just as Andre did."

The sheriff had the phone now. "Emil? Emil, you get down here right now, you hear?"

What would have happened if Emil had not decided to run for it is difficult to say. Veronica was not at all happy with what her detectives had accomplished. The plans she and Emil had made to spend half the year in the cabin would never be fulfilled, not with Emil indicted, convicted, and imprisoned for the murders of Art Fielding and Susan Wambach. Having directed the supposedly irate husband to the cabin, Emil followed him out, and, after Andre drove off, entered the cabin, shot Art and Susan with separate pistols and then arranged the bodies to look like a suicide pact. It was decided not to indict Veronica as an accomplice. She seemed genuinely surprised that it had been Emil and not Andre who had removed the obstacle to future bliss. Emil had neglected to tell her he had gone out to the cabin himself that fateful day.

"I can't say I'm glad the way this came out," the sheriff said when they were about to leave.

"I don't blame you," Phil said. "If it hadn't been for Roger . . .'"

But Roger would have none of that. "Let credit go where credit is due."

"And who is that?"

Roger looked at the sheriff and Phil with astonishment.

"Why, Fetch of course. If Fetch hadn't hid that shoe and those guns . . ."

"Come on, Roger," Phil said. "We've got a long drive ahead of us."

"Fetch?" the sheriff was saying as they left. "Fetch?"

7

Plum Lines[7]

Laila Davenport was given the news of her husband's murder when she emerged from the club where she had been playing bridge for the past three hours. Her reaction, given this concentrated use of the mind over an extended period of time, was delayed, but then she grasped what was being told her, let out a cry, and staggered into the arms of her playing partner, Freddy McNaughton.

The newly begotten widow was taken to her car, where she huddled sobbing in the back seat, from time to time looking beyond the gathering gawkers at Freddy, who was being given such details of the murder as were then known.

Guido Davenport's car had been parked in its special place in the garage from which he could pass directly into the building where his offices were. He had arrived at his office at 9:30; he had left again

7 A Roger Knight Mystery, by Ralph McInerny, Crisis Magazine, September 1997

shortly before noon, off for a luncheon engagement with a client, Manley Biran. The explosion that shredded Davenport's Mercedes had taken out two other luxury cars, caused damage to a dozen others, and had rained debris on terrified pedestrians below for some minutes. In the smoldering ruins of the car had been found Davenport's briefcase and his shockproof watch. His own remains would be more difficult to identify.

Freddy conveyed all this to Laila when he joined her in the car and drove her to her apartment. She leaned on his arm as they entered the building, but when the doors of the elevator closed on them, Laila and Freddy threw themselves into one another's arms. They emerged flushed and panting on the seventh floor, where Freddy hummed with impatience as Laila unlocked the door. Inside the apartment, the phone was ringing insistently.

"Ignore it," Freddy urged.

But it would have taken a stronger character than Laila's to resist the ringing of a telephone. She picked it up.

"Laila? This is Guido. An incredible thing has happened."

The phone slipped from Laila's fingers as she slipped to the floor. Freddy, hearing the voice of Guido on the phone, managed not to faint. He let himself out of the apartment and took the stairs to street level. Behind the wheel of his car, he hesitated before turning the ignition key, and when he did his eyes were squeezed shut. But a twist of the key had no more surprising effect than starting the motor and he drove off, relieved if confused.

When he was contacted by Guido Davenport, Philip Knight was inclined to accept the task of finding out what exactly had happened to the supposedly dead man who wished to employ him. Davenport had decided to retain his deceased status until he learned who it was who had wished him out of the world. He had, he hinted, some ideas as to who it might be. With his brother Roger ensconced in his swivel chair in the back of the van, able to while away the miles on his computer, Philip drove to Indianapolis, signed them into a hotel and telephoned Guido Davenport at the number he had been given.

"I'll be there in minutes."

"You're in the hotel?"

"It's as good a hideaway as any."

The bearded man with hair growing over his collar, wearing a sweat shirt and jeans, was not Philip's image of the prosperous criminal lawyer he and Roger had researched before starting out from their home in Rye.

"Only my wife knows I was not in that car," Davenport said, with a grim smile. "Whoever tried to get me could try again."

"A disgruntled client?"

"Or a gruntled rival. Those I represent are ruthless."

"Wodehouse," Roger said delightedly, recognizing the provenance of gruntled.

"I am an addict."

"Wouldn't it be wiser to put all this in the hands of the police?" Philip asked impatiently.

Davenport's expression was bleak. "I have stopped trusting anyone since this happened."

"Tell us what happened," Roger said. "On the day you were killed."

Davenport had arrived at his office at midmorning, having parked his car where he always did. It was unattended until almost three hours later when he left for lunch.

"Did you keep your luncheon appointment?"

"Eventually, yes."

When he entered the passageway leading to the garage, someone had hurried up beside him and snatched his briefcase. He was thrown to the ground and then the lights went out.

"I came to with my head pounding. I glanced at my watch but it wasn't there. Disoriented, I went back to my office."

"Whom did you see?"

"My secretary had gone to lunch. The office was empty."

"So you went off to lunch with Manley Biran."

Davenport looked from Roger to Phil. "I think you know I didn't."

"What we know is that Biran denied having a luncheon engagement with you."

Davenport rubbed his head and looked around the room. "My suite is very much like this one. How like a cell it has become." He inhaled. "I am ashamed of what I must now tell you. Laila has been so wonderful through all this. I had an engagement with another woman: Prossy Hirsh, the wife of a man serving a sentence in Michigan City."

"A client?"

Guido nodded. "He thinks I let him down. He is

not entirely wrong. The sting of defeat was made bearable by the relationship I had begun to establish with Prossy." He looked at Roger. "She likes Wodehouse. So few women do."

"That's no excuse." But Roger seemed to have hesitated.

"And now you think the explosion was Hirsh's revenge?" Philip was intent to keep them on track.

"Of course I do."

"But who started your car?

"Whoever mugged me in the passageway to the garage."

The explanation posed a problem, unless it was an appeal to pure accident. Whoever had arranged for Davenport's car to explode when the engine was started would hardly have hopped into the driver's seat and turned the key.

Roger said, "Did the mugger take your keys?"

For answer, Davenport fished forth from his pocket a jangling bouquet of steel. The three men pondered the significance of that, but it was Roger who suggested that the explosive had been detonated by a remote device, not the key, operated by someone who could see a man get into the car.

"The main thing is they think they accomplished their goal."

"Only Laila and I know they failed."

"You haven't been in touch with Prossy?"

Davenport raised a hand, his fingers twisted in the Scout salute. "No."

"I want to talk to Laila."

"I'll have her come here."

But Roger suggested it might be better if they called on her. "And several others. How far is Michigan City?"

"What's the point of talking to Hirsh? He has a perfect alibi."

"Who else would have a motive?"

Davenport looked sad as a roll of names scrolled past his mind's eye. "The aim of the criminal attorney is not to make friends. He ends up making enemies on both sides of the law. Of course it pays well."

"It was Gunther, you can be sure of it. He is a low, vindictive man." Prossy Hirsh said this of her husband with some satisfaction, but then what woman would be unmoved by the fact that one man had tried to kill another because of her? "He is insanely jealous."

"Why insane if he has reason?"

"Do you think he was faithful to me?"

"You make him sound like a man whose legs you have to count to make certain he isn't a goat."

Prossy Hirsh was confused. "Oh, maybe he's faithful now, while he's in prison. But what am I supposed to do. Wither on the vine?"

"I had an aunt who collected dry seaweed. I sometimes thought she lived entirely for pleasure."

Prossy dismissed this. "Gunther in prison and Guido blown up to kingdom come. Honestly."

"If your husband had arranged to do away with Guido, how would he go about it?"

"Haven't you read the papers?"

"I meant who would his cohorts be?"

"Oh, he never told me anything about his work."

"Who looks after his nightclub?" The Waikiki had been mentioned in newspaper accounts as the place where Davenport was supposed to lunch.

"Manley Biran." She sighed. "I don't know what I would have done without him."

Roger left her doubtful that she ran any risk of withering on the vine, but when he met Manley Biran he was once more baffled by the female psyche. Biran's face had the look of a fist whose clenched fingers concealed his eyes. Nonetheless Roger felt that he was being inspected carefully by the man who sat behind the desk in the manager's office of the Waikiki.

'You're fat."

"So are you."

"But I'm tall."

"Maybe I'll grow."

"Sideways. What do you want?"

"I am a private investigator looking into the death of Guido Davenport."

"You represent the insurance company?"

"If Davenport died as the result of violence he himself had incited we may not be liable."

This remark would have been difficult to justify in moral theology strictly construed. Roger was taking advantage of Biran's assumption that he was investigating Davenport's death for an insurance company. The fact that he and Philip would not be liable no matter how Davenport had died, and the further fact that Davenport was as alive as Manley Biran, did not make his remark less misleading.

"It wasn't Hirsh. Believe me."

Oddly enough, perhaps, Roger did believe him. When he got back to the hotel, he found Philip on the phone, speaking with great urgency. Phil pointed at the telephone which was turned on but muted. Roger punched the remote and listened to the announcement of the death of Mrs. Laila Davenport. He exchanged a look with Philip, who was hanging up the phone.

"He's not in the hotel. The police have learned that he has been holed up here. Apparently Laila told them that her husband did not die in that explosion."

Roger nodded. "Where do you think Guido is?"

"He said he was going to keep a rendezvous with his wife."

"I wonder if he did."

The police did not wonder. They were waiting for Guido when he returned to the hotel. Roger and Philip sat with him during the original interrogation.

"She didn't show up," Guido said, when asked if he had met his wife.

"Do you know why?"

Perhaps it is easier to look innocent with a beard. In any case, Roger had difficulty imagining a more innocent expression than that which Guido Davenport turned on his questioners. The police were unimpressed, not least because they felt that Guido had pulled a fast one on them by pretending to be dead for weeks. Their view was that Guido, incensed that Laila had told the police and suspecting that she wanted to enjoy his wealth without being encumbered by him, had killed her.

"I hate it when a client tries to exploit me," Phil said.

"How so?"

"I think we were meant to be his alibi."

Philip, in short, shared the police view that Guido had done away with Laila.

"How did she die?" Roger asked.

"A pillow over her face."

At two the following morning Roger shook his brother awake. Philip took some time focusing his mind.

"I think I know what happened, Phil."

"Tell me in the morning."

"I don't think we should wait."

"Wait for what?"

"To pay a call on Freddy McNaughton."

"Who in blazes is Freddy McNaughton?"

"In the phrase of the newspaper account, Laila Davenport's playing partner."

There are two kinds of criminal, the brazen and the craven. Freddy McNaughton was the latter sort. He could not bring himself to believe that the guilt he felt was invisible to others. When the Knight brothers interrupted his insomniac pacing of his apartment and identified themselves as private detectives, Freddy went to pieces. He could not spill out his story fast enough. The plan to blow up Guido had been no idea of his. He had gone along with Laila with a sense of disbelief that such a thing could actually be done. She assured him that contacts with Guido's clients enabled her to arrange for the fatal explosion.

"The man who mugged Guido went up with the car?"

Freddy tried to nod in such a way as to keep it a secret from his head. "He was supposed to drag Guido to the car and drive him away. He didn't know about the explosion."

"Laila gave him a key to the car?"

"Yes. As soon as we got back to her place, Guido called."

"You knew he was alive?"

"I heard his voice. Laila fainted. I fled. We talked on the phone, she wouldn't stop calling, but today was the first time I saw her since that awful day. I kept expecting Guido to come for me. I lived in terror. She said the only solution was to do ourselves what the explosion had failed to do."

"So you killed her?"

"I held a pillow over her face, to shut her up. She was taunting me, telling me I had to kill Guido."

Thus it was that the Knight brothers learned what the reader has known from the beginning.

"Freddy McNaughton," Guido said, shaking his head. "I can't believe it."

"Where were you when Freddy was killing your wife?"

Guido looked sheepish. He had been unable to

keep away from Prossy Hirsh. His rendezvous had been with her. Roger grew serious.

"There is something I have to tell you. She does not know Wodehouse at all. She did not respond to two of the more famous Wodehousian witticisms. No true fanatic would have failed to recognize them."

Guido reeled under this blow, but quickly regrouped. There was more to Prossy Hirsh's attractiveness than her supposed predilection for Wodehouse. He was, in the words of the Master, a man capable of only one idea at a time – if that. The arrest of Prossy as well as Freddy McNaughton brought Guido to his senses. His wife and her lover had tried to kill him and then her paramour killed Laila. It was enough to make a man wonder about the human race. Roger assumed the wise pensive look of the Oldest Member.

"Go golfing," Roger suggested. "It will make you forgiving of others."

8

A Lost Lady[8]

Lowndes had found the note in a volume he had picked up in a used bookstore and brought it to the attention of the Knight brothers. Philip settled for Lowndes' account of the note's message but Roger was still studying it with undisguised interest.

"It is what a dealer might list under *curiosa*, Roger."

"I wonder how long it was there," Roger murmured.

"Here's the book." The book was a first edition of Willa Cather's *A Lost Lady* and was in mint condition, another catalogue term, the metaphor apt enough since coins had been struck long before books were printed.

"Read the note aloud, Roger," Philip suggested.

"'When you read this I will be dead. This will make you feel superior, but you too are mortal. For God's

8 A Roger Knight Mystery, by Ralph McInerny, *Crisis* Magazine, October 1997

sake, repent of what you have done so my bodily death is not the cause of the death of your soul.'"

Lowndes and Philip traded theories on what the note might mean but were soon in agreement that the writer was addressing someone responsible for her death.

"Her death?" Roger asked.

"Look at the inside cover."

But Roger had already seen the ostensible owner's name, Margaret Trimble, Rye, 1923. That was the date of the book's publication; this was a first edition; presumably Margaret was the book's original owner.

"But of course you found it in a used book store."

"Raffles."

"How many owners might it have had?"

"It's in pretty good condition."

"Did you check to see who Margaret Trimble was?"

"And spoil your fun?"

There were no Trimbles in the Rye phone book, an unprepossessing volume. But of course it had been the out-of-the-wayness of Rye and the reduced and stately pace of life there that had attracted the Knight brothers when Philip had decided he had enough of the modern city. His livelihood depended on the misbehavior of men but he preferred to see Original Sin as productive of problems to be solved rather than a daily menace. Neither were there Trimbles in the vicinity. Roger settled down to his computer to see how far back in the layers of time one must go to find Trimbles in Rye. In a turn-of-the-century town directory an Arnold Trimble was listed as living at 302 Maple.

"Where's Maple?" Philip asked.

"It seems no longer to exist."

"Do streets die?"

"Are buildings razed? Do cities fall and then disappear under silt and debris, awaiting the arrival of an archeological team?"

"I thought only men were mortal."

"Only partly, Philip. As Margaret Trimble suggested to her addressee." This only made Philip uncomfortable. Roger was a genius, so his conversion to Catholicism could not be attributed to stupidity. But neither did Philip consider himself stupid for not understanding it. Of course he knew that Roger considered it only a matter of time before Philip too became a Catholic.

Strange as the notion of survival after death seemed, it had its attractions. On the other hand, Margaret Trimble's note suggested that the next life need not be a happy one.

A tall man in the courthouse, whose massive mustache seemed compensation for his egg-bald head, welcomed Roger's inquiry with the eagerness of a clerk whose services are seldom made use of. His name was Poussiere and he spoke incessantly as he scattered plat books and old maps on the large tables in his domain.

"There are still Oak and Elm and Walnut and Fir. Of course there was a Maple."

"What happened to it?"

"Progress." But Poussiere spoke the word with contempt. "The first courthouse was on Maple."

The building they were in was more than a century old, but it turned out to be the new courthouse, at least as time was computed by Poussiere. "There were some protests at the time. I have files. But the sense of the preciousness of the past was still the majority view." He had fetched a folder and was now dealing newspaper clippings onto the table. Roger, impressed by Poussiere's devotion to his job, looked at them. He was glad Phil had not come in. He would not have had the patience for this.

The original courthouse and eventually three blocks of what would now be called inner-city housing were sacrificed to the Maxwell Department store and the new boulevard that accommodated trolley tracks in its center and made Maple Street and the residences that had lined it things of the past.

"Maxwell?" Roger asked.

Poussiere folded his arms and looked at the ceiling. "It's being used now as a center for the homeless but scheduled to be knocked down in its turn." Poussiere sighed. "Once cities fell to natural disaster or military defeat. Now they are undone by their own citizens. Imagine a European city subject to such depredations."

Roger might have reminded him of what Hausmann had done to Paris or Mussolini to Rome, but he took the archivist's point.

"Maxwell's fled the city for the mall, first chance they had."

Roger frowned. "Is there a Maxwell's store at the mall?"

"More irony. They were bought out by a Canadian chain that went bankrupt. What you will know as Taylor's is the Maxwell store that was."

"You certainly know a lot about it.'"

Poussiere smiled away the compliment.

"My mother was a Maxwell."

"Was?"

"She died a year ago."

"May she rest in peace."

Poussiere obviously appreciated the sentiment. He actually shook Roger's hand. "There are not many of us left."

"How many?"

"Only one who still bears the name, My Uncle Drew."

"Drew Maxwell?"

"He is a resident at Oak Rest."

"To think that I came here to check up on Trimbles."

"Trimble! My grandfather married a Trimble."

"Margaret?"

"No. Maureen. Margaret was her sister."

"Tell me about the Trimble family."

"If you visited Uncle Drew you could ask him." This was clearly a ruse to get visitors for his uncle at the rest home. Roger suspected that Poussiere knew all about the Trimbles. But he took up the suggestion willingly. How often does one have an opportunity to satisfy his curiosity and perform a corporal work of mercy at the same time?

It is with old people as it is with babies, they all
look alike at first, but the seeming sameness of the
aged conceals very different lifetimes of experience.
The differences are further disguised by the egalitari-
an regime of a nursing home. There was little to dis-
tinguish Drew Maxwell's suite from those of others
who were in the penultimate stage of Oak Rest's services. Patients were allowed as much autonomy as they
could handle until daily medical care became a neces-
sity. One difference about Maxwell's apartment was
that no roar of television came from it. The old man
sat in casual clothes, at a desk. His expression was
impassive as he watched Roger waddle across the
room to him.

"How much do you weigh?" Maxwell asked as he
took Roger's hand.

"Too much."

"You'll never live to my age, carrying that kind of
weight around."

"I do as little carrying as possible."

The face seemed to crack into a smile. "I am told
you have been asking about me."

"It began because of my curiosity about the
Trimbles."

"My wife is a Trimble."

"That's why I'm here."

"She was a wonderful woman."

"I'm sure she was," Roger said, lowering himself
onto a sofa with a great sigh.

"Even so, it was seldom that it was my relation to
her rather than vice versa that interested people." He
said it simply as a matter of fact.

"And her sister was Margaret?"

Maxwell pressed backward in his chair.

"How do you know all these things."

"Most of them I found out when I spoke to your nephew at the court house."

"Grand nephew. Why did you question him?"

Looking at the solidity of the old man, his heavy upper body, the bald head set like a boulder on his broad shoulders, Roger had the sense that the whim-sicality of his pursuing a note found in a second-hand book would be met with incomprehension by Maxwell.

"Have you ever read a book called *A Lost Lady?* It was written by Willa Cather."

Maxwell stared at Roger.

"It's a novel."

"I never read novels. Never did."

"A copy of the novel was recently bought in a local second-hand bookstore. The copy belonged to Margaret Trimble."

"Margaret was a reader. She was a dreamer."

"Was she younger or older than you?"

The bullet head went back and forth. "We were the same age."

"You and Margaret Trimble?"

"Perhaps I was a year older."

"And you married her sister Maureen?"

"I did."

"A note was found in the book." Maxwell waited for Roger to say more. Roger took the note from his pocket and unfolded it. Maxwell followed this action warily.

"Is that it?"

"Yes."

"What does it say?" Roger heaved himself to his feet and gave the note to Maxwell, standing before him while he studied it. His lips moved as his eyes scanned the note. Then he read it again. He turned the sheet over and looked at the opposite side, then read the legend again, half aloud.

"This doesn't look old enough to be genuine."

"The book too is in very good condition," Roger said.

"This is her handwriting."

"You're sure?"

"Quite sure. We were close, Margaret and I. For several years. When we were young, we were engaged."

"But you married her sister."

"Time had elapsed, of course.

"You should sit down again," Maxwell said, but he did not offer to return the note.

"She never sent this," he said, when Roger was settled again on the sofa.

"To whom would she have sent it?"

The old man's eyes seemed to look at him from a century back.

"To me." Two words, two syllables, but they were wrung from the depths of the man's soul.

Roger let the silence develop after this surprising remark. The note was addressed to someone the writer regarded as her assassin. The clock on Maxwell's desk became audible, seeming to mock rather than record the passage of time. When Maxwell spoke again his tone was sepulchral.

"I do not read novels, but there is a line of poetry I remember. 'Each man kills the thing he loves.'"

"Oscar Wilde. 'The coward does it with a kiss, the brave man with a sword.'"

"I was a coward, but I learned to be brave."

"If the note were meant for you, she says you are responsible for her death."

His body heaved with a dry laugh. "Margaret was given to such excessive remarks. She reacted badly when I proposed to Maureen. Margaret and I had not seen one another for more than a year. Margaret had changed, but Maureen – she was Margaret as she had been, as I had loved her."

"She took your marriage badly?"

"Didn't young Poussiere tell you?"

"Tell me what?"

"She disappeared a few days before the wedding date. Gone without a trace. Of course the wedding had to be postponed. I assumed that was what she had intended. But after some months, Maureen and I married."

"You never saw Margaret again?"

"It was more difficult for Maureen than it was for me."

Roger told Philip and Lowndes what he had learned. Maxwell had given up the note reluctantly when Roger explained that it did not belong to him.

"You should have let him keep it." Lowndes said.

"I'll give it to him, if you like."

But a call to Oak Rest the following day informed him that Drew Maxwell was indisposed. Bedridden. This continued to be the case for several days. On the third day, when he and Philip were out in the van, Roger suggested that they stop where the former Maxwell Department store was being razed. That is why they were there when the body was found.

It was the remains of a woman whose neck had been broken. The bones were found when the wrecking ball swung into a wall, which burst and revealed is grisly occupant, sealed behind plaster for God knew how long.

"It must have happened when the building was under construction," Philip Knight said to Roger.

"Only her neck was broken."

Philip shook his head at the general mystery of life. "The wrecking ball could have done that."

Roger reminded him of his conversation with Drew Maxwell.

"Philip, I wonder if this could possibly be the missing Margaret Trimble."

"The woman who wrote the note Lowndes found in that book?"

"*A Lost Lady.*"

"Would the sister have been distraught enough to do herself in?"

"Or the bridegroom distraught enough to kill her?"

In the event, the identification of the remains could only be approximate. The dental records, fingerprints, the usual means were not available. Poussiere gave blood and a DNA expert gave it as his opinion that Poussiere was related to the woman whose remains had been found sealed in a wall of the Maxwell building. When Roger returned to Oak Rest he learned that Drew Maxwell had been moved to intensive care. A stroke had immobilized him. He was conscious but could not speak. His large eyes clung to Roger when they were left alone.

"Margaret's body has been found."

Maxwell's eyes closed, then opened. Roger took his hand.

"They think she killed herself."

No reaction.

"Or was killed." Roger leaned forward. "The brave man with a sword . . ."

Maxwell's hand exerted pressure on Roger's.

"Would you like to see a priest?"

A long minute went by and then Maxwell squeezed Roger's hand.

Roger told Father Rowan that the old man could respond to questions with pressure of his hand.

"He wants to go to confession? I didn't know he was Catholic."

"He just remembered himself."

Lumbering down the polished floor of the hallway toward double doors leading to the land of the hale and hardy, Roger considered that the wish expressed in Margaret's note was being realized at last. Soon, please God, Drew and Margaret, and Maureen too, would all be together where men and women are not given in marriage.

}100{